When
the
Sergeant
Came
Marching
Home

When the Sergeant Came Marching Home

the

DON LEMNA

Holiday House / New York

To Deanna

Text copyright © 2008 by Don Lemna
Illustrations copyright © 2008 by Matt Collins
All Rights Reserved
Printed in the United States of America
www.holidayhouse.com
First Edition
1   3   5   7   9   10   8   6   4   2

Library of Congress Cataloging-in-Publication Data
Lemna, Don, 1936-
When the sergeant came marching home / by Don Lemna ;
illustrations by Matt Collins. —1st ed.
p. cm.
Summary: In 1946 when his father returns from the war, a ten-year-old boy
and his family move from the Montana town where they had been living
to an old, run-down farm in the middle of nowhere, where they work hard
trying to make ends meet.
ISBN-13: 978-0-8234-2083-4 (hardcover)
[1. Farm life—Montana—Fiction. 2. Family life—Montana—Fiction.
3. Montana—History—20th century—Fiction.]
I. Collins, Matt, ill. II. Title.
PZ7.L53766Wh 2008
[Fic]—dc22
2007022424

Contents

When
the
Sergeant
Came
Marching
Home

CHAPTER ONE
Our Father Comes Home

Early in the summer of 1946, an infantry sergeant returned from the war and ruined my life by forcing me to move from our comfortable basement apartment in Wistola, Montana, out to a farm in the middle of nowhere.

It all began one day in the spring, when a letter arrived from across the sea. After Mother read it, she swept us into her arms and nearly hugged us to death.

"Your father is coming home," she said.

"Why are you crying?" Pat asked her.

"Because I'm so happy," she said.

Pat was not satisfied with this answer. Later on, after she'd let us go, he asked me about it.

"Women cry when they're happy," I told him.

"Why?"

"Because they're women," I explained.

At this point he lost interest in the conversation, and so did I.

A half hour later we were in the junkyard behind Mr. Kip's store, next door to our apartment block. Pat was squatting on top of an old icebox. I was below him, sitting halfway down inside the wooden barrel of an old hand-powered washing machine. My legs dangled over the side of it.

"What will it be like?" he asked me.

"What will what be like?"

"When we have a father," he said.

"We've always had a father," I informed him. "He's just been away in the war, that's all."

"What was he doing in the war?" Pat asked.

"Shooting Nazis," I said. I could have told him that our father landed on Omaha Beach in the second wave and fought the Nazis all the way across France and into Germany and was promoted to sergeant. But this would have been too much information for him to handle at one time.

Uncle Max out on the farm had fought in the war too, but he came home early, after a Nazi grenade wounded him in the rear end.

"Will he look like the guy in the picture?" Pat asked.

"He *is* the guy in the picture," I said, shaking my head in despair.

Pat was only six, and he knew very little about what

was going on around him. I was ten, and I knew pretty well everything.

"Who won?" he asked.

"Won what?"

"The war," he said.

I could hardly believe my ears.

"Do you see any Nazis around?" I exploded.

"No."

"Well, then, we must have won, because if we'd lost, we'd have Nazis all over the place!"

"Oh," he said. Even to him, it made sense. Then another look came into his eyes.

"I have to go to the bathroom," he said.

After he'd left, I let myself slip right down into the washing machine tub, my rear end leading the way. It was not an easy thing to do. I had to bend my legs at strange angles in order to get them wrapped around the oddly shaped wooden washing paddle. But somehow I managed it and sank down to the bottom of the tub. However, I soon discovered that it was very uncomfortable and decided to get out of there before it was too late. But it was already too late. I couldn't move, because my legs had both gone to sleep. I finally rocked back and forth until the tub tipped over and spat me out onto the ground.

Milton was standing there. Milton was my best friend. He stared at me as I got to my feet.

"I got stuck in it," I explained.

He nodded. He understood. He'd done the same thing himself.

"Sherry and Bobby are waiting," he said.

Sherry and Bobby were my other friends. We all lived in apartments in the Norris block, which definitely did not have bedbugs. It was the Dakota block down by the Roxy Theater that had them.

Every morning during the summer holidays the four of us—Milton, Bobby, Sherry, and me—went up and down the back alleys of Wistola, pulling our old steel-wheeled wagon along behind us, looking for things we could sell—mainly beer bottles. Our objective was always the same. To make enough money every morning so we could go to the movies every afternoon.

It cost ten cents for each of us to get into the movies, so we needed to make forty cents every day. But it wasn't hard to do. There were lots of beer bottles around, and we got ten cents a dozen for them. And sometimes we got really lucky. One day, behind Garbetts Business College, we found a typewriter that we sold to Mr. Kip for a dollar. Mr. Kip owned our junkyard and the secondhand store in front of it.

About a month after the letter from across the seas arrived, Mother received a Western Union telegram.

"Your father's coming home next Tuesday!" she cried. "He's coming into Great Falls on a troop train." And, once again, she took us in her arms and nearly squeezed us to death.

She borrowed Uncle Max's car, and very early Tuesday morning, we headed for Great Falls to meet him at the train station. It was a lovely morning. The sky was solid blue from end to end.

To help make the time go by, she told us stories about him—about how he'd been a policeman before the war and had patrolled the streets on the Wistola police bicycle, protecting citizens from criminals and making sure that little boys and girls didn't ride double on their bicycles.

When we finally got to Great Falls, we discovered that there was a huge crowd at the station.

We had to wait for a long time. When the train came in sight, cheers went up from everyone. I personally cheered my head off.

"You can stop anytime now," Mother said.

I was the first to spot him. He was standing on the bottom step of one of the coaches as the train glided slowly to a stop. I recognized him immediately from the picture.

"There he is!" I cried.

He swooped down on us, and he hugged our mother and kissed her. He lifted Pat high up in the air and kissed him. He lifted me up and hugged me until I could hardly breathe, then he kissed me on the cheek.

I was amazed at how big and tall and strong he was. I was very happy and excited. We all were.

He had a knapsack on his back and, later on that afternoon, we discovered that it contained a bunch of Baby Ruth chocolate bars, a shaving kit, a small pile of French coins, and many other things of interest, including a beautiful black gun.

The gun was the last thing he revealed to us up in the hotel room. It was wrapped in oiled white linen, and I nearly had a conniption fit when he unwrapped it and showed it to us.

"It's a German Luger," he informed us.

I recognized the gun. I'd seen it in the hands of Nazis in many of the movies I'd watched over the last three years. But I never dreamed the day might come when I would actually hold a real one in my hands.

Our father told us he'd bought it from a defeated German soldier for a pack of cigarettes. He let me pick it up, and it weighed a ton and a half. I could barely hold it steady.

"You're not supposed to bring those things back," Mother said, raising her eyebrows. "How did you get it past the customs?"

"I hid it in a loaf of bread," he said with a laugh. "Everyone in the company had one. You've never seen so many loaves of bread going ashore at the same time."

He even had bullets for it. They were cleverly concealed inside a hollow black shoelace. The shoelace weighed a ton.

I was thrilled with the gun and wanted him to let me shoot it right away, without delay. But he only laughed at me.

"When you've finished high school, you can shoot it," he said. "If your marks are good," he added.

A major disappointment that was. I'd only just passed into grade five.

We had two glorious days in Great Falls. We stayed in the Rainbow Hotel and ate in restaurants and went to a movie. But after we returned to Wistola, we saw very little of him. He was gone pretty well from morning to night. When I asked my mother where he went, she looked down at me and smiled.

"He's looking for a farm," she said. "He's not a man to waste time when he's after something."

"Oh," I responded.

One morning I saw him take out his pocket watch to check the time. It glinted in the sunlight coming through the window.

"Is that made of gold?" I asked.

"Well, the case is gold," he said.

"Is it real gold?"

"Yes, it's real gold," he said.

"Did you get it from the war?" I asked.

"No, but it went through the war with me," he said.

"Where did you get it?" I persisted.

"It was my father's—your grandfather's. It went to war with him too, the First World War. His lieutenant sent it back to my mother when he was killed at Cantigny."

I remembered the picture of that grandfather in the old album. I'd seen it many times. He had a large mustache, and there was a vase of flowers on a stand behind him.

"My mother gave it to me on my eighteenth birthday, and I've kept it in my pocket ever since," he said. "I wouldn't feel right if it weren't there."

He handed it to me, and I was surprised by the weight of it. I looked it over carefully and handed it back to him.

He stared at the watch, and there was a faraway look in his eyes.

"This watch is all that's left of him," he said.

One day he came home in the middle of the afternoon and led us out to the front of the apartment block to show us a surprise.

"There she be," he said.

He was pointing at an ancient one-ton Ford truck parked at the curb in front of us.

"She's ours," he said proudly. "I bought her this morning."

He took us for a ride right then, and the old truck lurched and swayed as it went down the streets. It had lots of power, however. I could feel its power vibrating all around me.

On one of the deserted streets, he stopped and put it into reverse. We then went backward up to the end of the block, and it was even more fun than going forward.

It was all very thrilling. We'd never owned a truck before. Nor a car. Nor anything at all, except that before the war he had a bicycle. I remembered that bicycle well, although I was only a baby. He took me for rides in it. I used to sit in a box that was fastened to the back fender, and I was transported down the streets. I remember looking up and seeing a canopy of green leaves high above me, gliding by. But that was a long time ago.

"I think I'll call her Maggie," Father said, thumping the

steering wheel with his big hands. "She feels like a Maggie to me."

Soon afterward we used Maggie to travel back to Great Falls, where we once again stayed in the Rainbow Hotel and ate our supper in a restaurant. The following morning Father changed into his uniform.

"Are you going back to the war?" Pat asked.

"The war's over," I said, despair in my voice. "Don't you know anything?"

"Your father's going to be in a parade," Mother gently explained. "That's why we've come here. For the parade. In a little while you'll see him marching down the street with all the other soldiers who were in the war."

"It's our victory parade," Father said with a smile.

Presently he left our room and, later on, the rest of us assembled out on the street, along with thousands of other people. After waiting out there for a while, we heard a band playing in the distance. It took a long time for it to get to us, but it was worth waiting for. It was a full Army marching band with drums and trumpets, and it was followed by long columns of marching soldiers.

"There he is!" Pat cried.

I saw him at the same time, marching in the front row of his column. He looked very fine. Mother began to cry a little, and Pat looked up at her.

"She's happy," I said, anticipating his question.

The parade was a great success, and we were all happy as we drove back to Wistola that afternoon. Everything seemed to be going along very well.

Then one day he came home and announced that he'd done it.

"Done what?" I asked.

"I've bought a farm," he said. "What do you think I've been doing ever since I got back?"

"Oh," I said.

We had a celebration that night, and the next morning he and Mother began to pack our dishes and things into cardboard boxes.

"What are you doing?" Pat asked them.

"We're getting ready to go to our new farm," Mother said.

"It's near a little town called Station Hill. Not far from your uncle Max's farm," Father said with a smile. "One square section."

I gave him a puzzled look. I really didn't understand what he was talking about. But then I suddenly understood.

"We aren't going to move!" I cried.

"What's the matter? You were happy about it last night," Mother said in her calm voice. She squatted down to my level and did up a button on my shirt as she spoke.

I had nothing against it last night; however, it had simply never occurred to me that they intended to go live on this farm of his. I couldn't believe it was happening.

"You're gonna love it out there," he said happily. "Fresh air. Freedom to roam!"

"It's not very far from here," Mother said soothingly. "And we'll come back for visits. I'm going to raise chickens and I'll sell the eggs in the market by the Dakota and you guys can come with me. You'll be able to go to the movies and see your friends every Saturday."

"It's got a creek on it," he said. "You can even swim in it, once it gets warm enough."

I looked at my mother with tears in my eyes. I couldn't believe what she was doing to me. I didn't want to leave Milton and all my other friends. I didn't want to leave Mrs. Clarke at Wistola Elementary. I didn't want to leave the downtown, with its two movie theaters and the popcorn man and Riverside Park and all the other excitements.

"Will there be some ducks?" Pat asked.

"We'll have ducks and chickens and all sorts of animals," Mother promised him. "As soon as we've had a chance to settle in," she added.

Pat's eyes brightened at the prospect, and I could scarcely believe it. He was willing to trade a good life in the city for a few ducks.

"I don't want to live on a farm," I groaned.

When I said this, my father's eyes became very hard and he looked down at me as if he were still a sergeant in the army.

"You'll do what you're told," the Sergeant said.

And that was the end of our happy relationship.

"I hate him!" I said to Pat when we were safely outside in the junkyard.

"Who?" Pat asked.

"Him," I said. "He's ruined my life."

"She says we can have five of them," Pat declared.

I looked at him.

"Ducks," he said.

I spent the rest of that day sulking all around the place. My life was over. But it made no difference to them. None at all. The very next day the Sergeant loaded all the furniture and boxes onto Maggie, and we left the city forever.

CHAPTER TWO
Horsepower

"The country is a great place for kids," he said as we drove out of the city. "You're gonna love it."

We drove across the countryside for what seemed like hours, until we came upon a little town. He drove into it and parked Maggie across the street from a store. "Zackary's General Store," the hand-painted sign said in big red letters.

"This is Station Hill," he said. "Our farm is about eight miles from here."

"This is where you'll be going to school in the fall," Mother informed us.

I shuddered at the thought. I didn't want to go to school here. The idea was frightening.

"In the meantime, who wants an ice-cream cone?" the Sergeant asked.

"I do!" Pat cried.

I did not give in. I said nothing. I was boiling with anger and hate.

"Well, them that does, come with me," the Sergeant said.

By the time they were halfway across the street, I felt I'd made my point. I got out of Maggie and followed them into the store.

Ice cream is a very soothing thing. As we drove out of Station Hill, all licking our ice-cream cones like mad, I even found myself getting a little curious about our new farm. The farms in the Roy Rogers cowboy movies were always very nice. If our farm was like one of those, then maybe it wouldn't be so bad.

I saw the farm long before we reached it. It was on the left side of the road, just a little way back from the bottom of a large hill. There were trees all around the yard, though mostly on the far side of the house. It looked pretty from a distance.

"It's got a real nice creek," the Sergeant informed us for the nineteenth time. "It runs right through the east quarters."

"Will there be ducks in it?" Pat asked.

"I don't know," he said. "Maybe in the fall."

"We'll have some nice tame ducks, don't you worry," Mother promised him. Her eyes were glowing. She was very happy.

14

As we came up the dirt road, we went past a large white farmhouse with a pack of girls playing outside, and then, through the trees up ahead, I got a glimpse of our new home. It was a two-story house, clad in brown shingles. In back of it there was a big red barn and a few other buildings. On one side of the yard, there was a small pond.

When we drove into the yard, I got out and looked more closely at the house and my heart fell into my boots. It was an old wreck. It looked like it had ghosts living in it. I looked around at the other buildings and saw that our new farm wasn't new at all! In fact, it was so old that I thought that we should let it die in peace and move back to Wistola. I wanted to tell the Sergeant this, too, but he was so happy that I was afraid to say anything against it.

Our "new" house didn't have any doors or windows to speak of, and a large flock of pigeons was living upstairs in our bedroom. The place was a terrible mess inside. There was dirt and dust all over.

"The Smiths haven't lived here for a few years, so it needs a little cleaning and fixing, but it'll be a fine home when we're finished with it," the Sergeant said as he led us into the living room.

"It'll be lovely," Mother declared. "And the best thing of all, it's ours! We'll never have to pay rent on it!"

"No," the Sergeant laughed. "Just the mortgage."

"What's a mortgage?" Pat asked.

"It's when you sell your soul to the devil," the Sergeant answered quickly.

"What's a soul?" Pat asked.

"It's the part of you that you can't see," I said, whereupon Pat began to examine the air around him.

Mother stepped across the room, and she tore a loose strip of green wallpaper off the wall.

"Good plaster behind it," the Sergeant said, looking at the bare wall where the wallpaper had been stripped away.

"Where's the light switch?" I asked, after looking around the room and not seeing one.

"They don't have electricity out here yet," the Sergeant informed me.

"No electricity!" I cried. "What about the radio?"

He just shook his head at me and smiled.

"No radio!" I cried. I felt a cold chill run through my body. Never again would I hear those thrilling words, "The shadow knows," followed by that insane laugh. There would be no more Fibber McGee and Molly, with things crashing out of the closet when Fibber opened the door. There would be no more Charlie McCarthy and Mortimer Snerd. No more Superman! No more Green Hornet! No more anything!

"Electricity will come out here someday," he said. "You have to have faith in the future."

The future? I had no future. Someday soon they would find me lying among the trees out back, and they would find me dead. Dead! Dead from an excess of boredom.

"What are you looking for?" Mother asked me a few minutes later, as I ran about the place with an urgent expression on my face, looking into closets and the pantry for what wasn't there.

"I can't find the bathroom," I confessed. I felt a bit of a fool, not being able to find it.

"Come with me," the Sergeant said.

He led me outside, onto the stoop, and pointed at a little building with a half-moon cut into the door.

"There's the bathroom," he said.

I should have known. It was an outhouse, exactly like the one at Auntie Margaret and Uncle Max's farm. And it had exactly the same kind of rough wood seat with the same two holes, above the same kind of awful poop pit that produced that same awful smell. My heart sank into my boots. In my mind's eye I saw again the wonderful modern bathroom in the Norris block, back in my beloved Wistola. A beautiful bathroom, fully equipped with sink, bathtub, and toilet. A beautiful bathroom that we had only had to share with six other families. I wished I'd appreciated it more. I wished with all my heart I could go back to it now, and I would have said so right then, but I couldn't talk freely when he was around. I hated him for ruining our lives!

From that first moment when Mother attacked the green wallpaper, they hardly ever stopped working. Uncle Max and Auntie Margaret's farm was about three miles away, and later on that morning, they appeared on the scene with their truck. They brought my cousin Annie with them, along with a huge basket of food.

Annie and Pat and I each took a sandwich and a bottle of Orange Crush and we had a picnic along the creek. After we finished our lunch, we wandered along the shallow waters for some distance, until I was bitten by a vicious mosquito.

"Where are you going?" Annie asked me.

"I'm going back. A mosquito bit me," I said.

"You are such a dunce!" Annie growled. "Come on, Pat."

On my way back I rubbed my arm where the mosquito had attacked me and I thought about what I'd be doing if I were back in Wistola. Right about now we'd be delivering our morning's beer bottles to the liquor store, and a little while from now, we'd be sitting in the Roxy, watching a movie. Maybe it would be a Tarzan movie with Johnny Weissmuller. But no. Instead I was out here in the middle of nowhere, being eaten alive by country mosquitoes.

After lunch the grown-ups began to work again, and they worked until dusk. And the next day was the same. They just never stopped. Day after day they worked at it. They cleaned and washed the place from top to bottom. The hole in the roof was repaired. Doors and windows appeared on the scene and went into place. Everywhere around there, there was the sound of scraping and hammering and sawing. The smell of fresh paint was always in the air.

As for us kids, we climbed through the barn and played in the hay and wandered along the creek, and it was almost like having fun. Well, maybe being out here was okay for a holiday, but it wasn't the sort of thing you can go on enjoying day after day.

For the first week we slept in the back of Maggie, under the stars. Auntie Margaret begged us to come home with them and stay there, but the Sergeant would not hear of it. After they'd gone home, he explained his reasons to our mother.

"I don't want to owe him anything," he said.

"It wasn't him that invited us," she responded coldly. "It was my sister."

"It's all the same," the Sergeant replied.

The truth of the matter was that the Sergeant and Uncle Max didn't get along all that well. In fact, they had a tendency to spend most of their free time arguing about one thing or another. Usually it was in a good-natured way, but sometimes they got downright angry with each other.

"Actually, I don't mind it so much," Mother murmured. "Sleeping in the open, I mean. It's a nice change, and the stars are pretty."

"I love the stars!" Pat chirped.

The Sergeant pointed out the Big Dipper and then various other star formations. I don't know what they were called. Pat was very enthusiastic about it all, but I had no interest in stars, since they were too far away to affect me. The Sergeant was still droning on about them when I fell asleep.

The day finally came when we transferred our furniture

across the yard, from the barn into the house, and that night we moved in with the mice.

I had always believed that there was nothing in the world that my mother was afraid of. She was not afraid to go after the people in the apartment block who failed to wash out the bathtub after they used it. She was not afraid to return bad meat to the butcher and bawl him out about it. She was not afraid of thunderstorms or vicious dogs. But I discovered she was deathly afraid of mice. She screamed at them whenever they came out to look at her, which they did quite often. I think they actually sensed that she was afraid of them. And once a mouse gets the idea you're afraid of him, he likes to come out and scare you whenever he has a free moment on his hands.

"I can't stand them!" she exclaimed one morning at breakfast, after a night that was full of small, scurrying activities.

"Hold on," the Sergeant said in that hearty manner he had. He then abruptly left the table, put on his cap, and went out the door.

"Where's he going?" Pat asked.

"Search me," Mother said with a shrug of her shoulders.

A half hour later, he came back with a mean-looking tomcat.

"I got him from a farmer down the road," he explained. "He'll take care of them."

Soon afterward Pat named the cat Cannibal, because of certain habits he had. And, shortly after that, the mice stopped coming out to look at Mother.

Of all the cats in the world, this old tomcat, Cannibal, was the sweetest of them all—except in regard to mice. But he loved people. He loved to curl up on people's laps, and he would head directly for any lap as soon as it came in sight. He also liked to have his head rubbed. In fact, you could rub it forever, even until the fur fell off, and he would still never get tired of it. He was an old cat and one of his ears was half gone, but he was still healthy and vigorous.

It turned out that there was an elderly horse living on our farm when we arrived. Pat and I found him out in the pasture beyond the woods. His name was Flight, and the Sergeant told us he was an old plow horse who had seen better days. He said Flight came with the farm and there-fore belonged to us.

One day, soon after we'd discovered Flight, I helped Pat to get up on his back and then stood back to see what was going to happen. Nothing happened. Flight just kept on eating grass like he'd been doing and didn't seem to notice Pat was riding him. I then got on his back too, and both of us spent an hour riding him, going nowhere.

In time we discovered that if we were willing to wait long enough, Flight would eventually begin to move with us on his back. However, we had no idea how to steer him, and so most of our journeys on Flight took us places we didn't want to go. Once we found ourselves far out on the southeast pasture, and after an hour of waiting and hop-ing, we decided that the only sure way to get back to the house in time for supper was by walking there.

After our long walk home from the far pasture, we complained bitterly to the Sergeant about Flight, and the next morning he showed us how to put a horse bit in his mouth—in Flight's mouth, that is. Once we had a bit and reins installed on him, steering Flight was simple. Very simple, in fact, since he would only go in one direction. To the left. He wouldn't make a right turn at all, unless one of us got off and pulled him around. Eventually we discovered that the whole trick with Flight was to decide where you wanted to ride him and then make sure it was on your left when you started out. Otherwise, you'd miss it.

The Sergeant used Flight quite a lot during those early days, because he was easy on gas. He used him to pull the cord wagon, and once he put a special harness on him, with chains attached, and Flight pulled the little red granary across the yard.

For some reason Flight took a fancy to Pat. When Pat was outside, he would sometimes come in from the pasture or the woods and follow him around. Sometimes we found him outside the house, waiting for Pat to come out.

"He likes you," the Sergeant said to Pat one morning when the horse came over to smell his hair.

"He likes me," Pat repeated.

"If he changes his mind, he could kill you with one kick," I pointed out.

Then I asked the Sergeant, "Could I have a dog?" I fully expected him to say yes, but once again he surprised and disappointed me.

"We'll have a dog someday," he said, "but it's not going to be some old mutt. I'm going to get a purebred German shepherd."

"When will we get him?" I asked.

"When I have enough to buy one," he said. "But right now money is in short supply. It doesn't grow on trees, you know."

I had a feeling then that I would never have a dog, for I knew we were very poor. He had spent everything we had to buy the farm and the truck. But that night, when I was sitting out on the stoop, I heard them talking about it in the kitchen, and my hopes rose up again.

"All he wants is a dog to keep him company," she said. "He's left all his friends behind. I don't see why . . ."

"I'm not going to have some mongrel running around the place," he said. "It's going to be a purebred German shepherd or nothing. Anyway, I've already told him that, and I can't go back on my word. If I did, he wouldn't respect me."

"Maybe not, but he might love you a little more," Mother said in an acid voice.

Sometimes we were forced to help our mother and the Sergeant, but at least it was something to do. And once, after Pat and I had delivered two pails of morning water from our windmill pump house to the kitchen, the Sergeant smiled at us and said we were doing fairly well for a couple of city slickers with soft hands. Pat usually spilled twice as much water as he delivered.

One morning during our second week on the farm, the Sergeant took us down the lane past the barn and showed us a building. Actually, we'd seen this building before. It was old and gray and it had an unpleasant air about it.

"This is the old henhouse," the Sergeant informed us.

We went inside, and it was really a mess. The floor was covered with chicken droppings and bits of rotten straw and lost feathers. The roosts were coated with the same stuff, and even the ceiling had chicken droppings on it.

"What does a hen look like?" Pat asked.

"It looks like a chicken," I quickly informed him, drawing from my deep reservoir of country knowledge.

"This is where your mother's going to keep her laying hens when we get them," the Sergeant said.

At that exact instant, my inner voice told me there was something about this chicken coop that I really didn't like. Then a deeper and more powerful voice told me what it was.

"I want you troopers to clean it up. Use the flat barn shovel and the wheelbarrow and get all this chicken crap out. All of it. Right down to the dirt floor. You can dump it beside those chokecherry bushes over there."

I looked at Pat, and Pat looked at me. Later, after the Sergeant had gotten us started and then left us to it, I said what was on our minds:

"I wish we still lived in Wistola," I moaned. Then I went over to the wall and kicked it, for I had already developed an intense hatred of chicken coops.

When Pat threw the first shovelful of dry chicken crap

into the wheelbarrow, a great cloud of dust rose up, and he disappeared from view. Then he disappeared altogether. When I looked around the corner, he was halfway to the house.

"Where are you going?" I yelled.

"I'm going to tell Mother on him!" he cried.

Not a bad idea, I thought, and I ran after him.

We found Mother in the kitchen, dripping with sweat. She was boiling the laundry. Pat immediately let out with a barrage of complaints about the hated chicken coop. I solemnly confirmed everything he said as he went along. It is not too farfetched to say that, in all of recorded history, no farm building has ever been subjected to such criticism and condemnation as that old chicken coop received from Pat and me that morning.

Eventually Mother came out with us and looked inside the chicken coop. Then she told us to wait there while she went to the barn to talk things over with the Sergeant.

"She's going to ask him to let us go," I told Pat. And my heart rose as I watched her head off. I had a lot of faith in Mother. She was very pretty with her red hair, and I knew that the big Sergeant liked her a lot.

As soon as she disappeared into the barn, Pat and I ran after her. We went in the back way and crawled up the ladder to the loft as quietly as possible. Soon we were lying on the floor a few feet above them, looking down through the cracks in the floorboards.

"They're really too young," I heard her say. "There's a foot of chicken manure in there, and I don't—"

"It won't hurt them," the Sergeant interrupted with a grunt. He was adjusting something in the engine of the old tractor while Mother was talking to him.

"It would be different if they were used to it," she said.

"They'll get used to it soon enough," he countered.

At this point I had an almost overwhelming urge to shout, "Come on, Mom!" I didn't, of course.

"Who's winning?" Pat whispered to me.

"I don't know," I whispered back.

"Really!" Mother exclaimed.

"Well, it's too late anyway," the Sergeant declared. "I told them to do it, and I can't go back on my orders."

"Well, I don't agree," Mother responded.

"Then I guess we'll have to leave it at that," the Sergeant said.

Mother then turned away in a huff and marched out of the barn. Even though I couldn't see her eyes, I knew they were flashing. Her eyes always flashed like neon lights when she got mad.

"Who won?" Pat whispered to me.

"Okay, you two! Get down from the loft and get back to work!" the Sergeant shouted from below.

"He won," I said to Pat.

Did I mention that his former occupation involved shooting people?

It really was terrible work.

"This is going to take us years and years," I said morosely as I watched how slowly Pat filled the wheelbarrow. Meanwhile, Cannibal settled down lazily in the grass to watch the proceedings.

Later on, as I wheeled the first load out to the bushes, the Sergeant drove by on his way to the field. He waved at us from the tractor and stuck his thumb up in the air. This, as I understood it, meant that he was happy because he got to ride the tractor and we got to do all the dirty work.

As soon as he was out of sight, we took a much-needed break. Flight then wandered over. He stood next to Pat and began to smell his hair. While Pat was rubbing his muzzle, I picked up a large rock and threw it at the chicken coop.

"Remember when Dad used Flight to pull that red building around?" Pat asked. "Maybe we could—"

"Shut up for a minute," I interrupted. "I'm thinking."

I don't know where my wonderful idea came from, but it struck me like a ton of bricks.

"We can use Flight to pull the chicken coop onto some clean ground!" I exclaimed. "Just like he pulled that other building! Then all the chicken crap will be left behind!"

It took a very long time to get the heavy harness on Flight and drag the chains out and attach them. Then it took another long time to get Flight moved around so he could reach the chicken coop by making left turns. We eventually got him there, but then it took a while to find good places to attach the chains to. I finally attached mine to a sturdy inside post on the left side of the door, and Pat attached his to the one on the right.

"Now we gotta do it real slow," I warned him as I pulled on the reins.

Flight was very obliging, at first. He moved steadily ahead until the chains tightened up. But then he refused to budge. We tried everything, but as soon as the chains tightened and the chicken coop began to creak a little, Flight stopped dead in his tracks.

"It isn't going to work," I said.

Pat wasn't listening. In fact, he was gone. Then I saw him come running out of the back of the barn with the old buggy whip in his hand.

"If we hit him with this, he'll go," Pat said.

"I'd better do it," I said, taking the whip from his hand. "You'll hit him too hard, and he might wreck it."

I then gave Flight a gentle tap on the rump with the buggy whip, just the merest touch.

It was, I think, very fortunate that Pat and I happened to be standing on Flight's right-hand side, because the moment the whip touched him, Flight lurched to the left like a maddened elephant. He tore everything loose that was holding him back and headed straight for the woods. The chains and the two doorposts went with him.

"It didn't work," Pat observed.

Then, behind us, the chicken coop slowly collapsed. It seems the doorposts were an essential part of what was holding it up. As the chicken coop came down, a great cloud of dust and feathers rose up and engulfed Pat and me.

"Where are you?" I asked.

"I don't know," Pat replied.

When the dust settled, we stared in horror at the devastation.

Where's Mother going to put her chickens? I wondered.

"Is he going to shoot us?" Pat asked, looking worriedly out at the field.

A moment later, we ran bawling back to the house. Mother met us on the doorstep.

"I saw it," she said, looking solemnly down at the two dirty little wretches she'd brought into the world.

We promptly threw ourselves on her mercy.

"It was Pat's idea!" I proclaimed.

"No, it wasn't!" Pat cried. "He did it. He hit Flight with a whip!"

"It doesn't matter whose fault it was. The problem is how you're going to explain it to your father when he comes back." She sighed.

"Can we move back to Wistola now?" Pat asked.

"Don't be silly," Mother replied. She shook her head at us and sighed again. "Maybe he'll think it fell down by itself, so don't tell him you pulled it with the horse."

She shook her head again, this time with her eyes closed. "In the meantime, I suggest you get the harness off Flight before your father gets back. Then come back here and get cleaned up."

Later in the day, the Sergeant returned from the field. We heard the tractor stop, and, a few minutes later, he came into the kitchen. Of course, Pat and I didn't notice him, since we were busy reading the *Children's Illustrated Bible* and couldn't look up. We both knew that Mother was at the stove and we both hoped she might protect us, as she'd always done in the past. Of course, in the past we'd hardly ever gotten into trouble with a Nazi shooter.

"I suppose you noticed," Mother said quietly. "The old chicken coop collapsed."

"I noticed," he said in a hard voice.

Pat and I were still reading with all our might, but we felt electricity in the air all around us.

"It's lucky the boys weren't in it when it happened," she said.

"Is it?" he asked.

"Really, dear, you can't trust those old buildings," she declared.

There was a long pause before the Sergeant replied.

"Well, I expect we can build another chicken coop," he said finally. "And maybe those two boys over there would give me a hand with it—that's if they can tear themselves away from the Bible for long enough."

We looked up at him.

"How about it, you two? Will you help me build a new one?" he asked us.

Pat and I agreed to this suggestion much as Moses accepted the Ten Commandments from God. That is, quickly, with a very powerful demonstration of enthusiasm and gratitude.

"What we'll do," he said with a slight smile, "is get Flight to help us pull the remains of the old one apart, and then we'll build a new one with the old boards."

"Good idea!" Mother exclaimed.

"And while I'm at it," the Sergeant said, "I'll show the boys how to put the work harness on Flight."

Mother and the Sergeant then began to laugh. Pat quickly joined in, even though he had no idea what he was laughing at. As for me, I refused to laugh at his joke.

CHAPTER THREE
Our Hermit

It was very hard work rebuilding the chicken coop. I was given the dirty job of cleaning the chicken dung off old boards with a metal scraper, and I hated it. After it was over I could no longer eat eggs, unless they were hard-boiled.

A few days later, the rebuilt chicken coop was full of chickens. There was also one rooster to wake us up in the morning, and there was a turkey with its own pen.

After the chickens were installed, Pat and I were obliged to go out to the chicken coop every morning and collect the eggs they'd laid during the night. I didn't like it much, but it wasn't a hard job. Besides, I was used to gathering things. I'd spent three years going up and down the back alleys of downtown Wistola gathering beer bottles.

I had always experienced a little drip of happiness whenever I found a beer bottle, and a bit of that feeling seemed to transfer itself to finding the eggs. I was a little afraid of the chickens at first, but it was not long before I realized that they were not as tough as they looked.

One Saturday morning, after the chickens were laying more eggs than we needed, Pat and I piled into Maggie and Mother drove us to Wistola. And while she sold her eggs at the market behind the Dakota block, Pat and I went to the Roxy with my friends to watch *Tarzan and the Amazons*.

The Amazons were a tribe of wild women who lived in a hidden city in the Mountains of the Moon, not far from Tarzan's bamboo tree house. They had a lot of gold. Tarzan was the only man they trusted, and they didn't trust him much either. It was a terrific movie. Had we still lived in Wistola, I would likely have seen it twice.

The light blinded me as I came out of the theater. But when I got used to it, I saw that Maggie was across the street with Mother sitting behind the driver's wheel, reading her book. Then I remembered I had to go back to that awful place.

"I sold all my eggs!" Mother exclaimed. "All of them! Just like that!"

She could hardly wait to get back to the farm and tell the Sergeant, and she laughed and sang most of the way there. As for me, I couldn't get rid of the sad image of Milton and Bobby and Sherry going up the alley behind the Woolworth building without me.

He had completely ruined my life. I was now reduced to feeding chickens and stealing their eggs. What next?

After we got home I wandered down to the creek by myself. I took off my shoes and socks and began to wade up the little stream. It was when I came to the corner at the dead tree, where the creek changed directions, that I made the decision. I decided I would escape from this hateful place.

I thought that if I could manage to save ten dollars, it would be enough to keep me for a while—at least until I was settled down in the new place. I did not intend to spend any of the money on traveling there. I would hitchhike all the way. At night I would sleep in ditches in order to save money. I would also take a large lunch with me when I left.

I already knew exactly where I would go. I would go to Hollywood, California, where all the movie stars live, and I would start my life over there. There was even the possibility that one of them would adopt me—or at least let me play with her dog and swim in her swimming pool from time to time. I would cut her lawn in return. If she had chickens, I would feed them and gather their eggs for her, in exchange for my meals.

It would not be easy leaving my mother, but I had to do it. Poor Mother. She would cry every night because she missed me. It's his fault, I thought. If you hadn't let him move us out here, it would never have happened.

In the meantime, until I had enough money to make a break for it, I would have to stay put and suffer. However, having made plans to escape helped me to endure. It gave me hope.

The day after our trip to Wistola, the Sergeant came storming into the house.

"What's wrong?" Mother asked him.

"We've got a squatter!" the Sergeant exclaimed. "I was talking to Schneider out on the road, and he told me there's an old hermit living along the creek, over at the far end of the southeast quarter. What's more, he's been living there for years!"

"I wonder why the Smiths never mentioned him when they sold us the place," Mother said calmly.

"I'll tell you why!" the Sergeant said loudly. "They didn't want to have to clear him out! Now I'll have to do it!"

"What's a hermit?" Pat asked.

"It's someone who prefers to live away from people," Mother said, which was close to what I was thinking.

"You two stay away from him," the Sergeant warned us, which was not very close to what I was thinking.

Mother smiled and put her hand on the Sergeant's shoulder.

"Couldn't we all just leave him alone?" she suggested. "He's not bothering anybody, and it's just bush and scrub pasture out there."

"That's not the point." The Sergeant frowned. "If I know he's there and I let him stay, he might have a legal claim to the land he's squatting on. So I have to give him the boot. I've got no choice."

"Really, darling, what's an acre, more or less?" Mother asked sweetly. "We've got four quarters."

"You don't understand," the Sergeant responded.

"I think I do," Mother replied in the bone-dry voice she used when she was miffed. "I understand quite well. You're going to throw an old man out of his home."

"No, I'm not!" the Sergeant said with determination. "He can take his home with him when he goes. But he's not squatting on my land!"

"Boys," Mother said, turning to us, "take your sandwiches and milk and eat outside."

We went out and sat below the kitchen window so that we could listen to them argue while we ate.

"What does a hermit do?" Pat asked.

"Don't ask me," I said.

After we'd finished our sandwiches, the argument was still sputtering along inside, so Pat and I went for a walk. When we reached the creek, we began to follow it to the southeast. It wandered this way and that way, in the irregular fashion that creeks seem to prefer, and the little wooded stream was full of small surprises: a tiny, babbling waterfall, a beaver dam with a pond behind it, an old man fishing in the pond . . .

"It's Santa Claus!" Pat whispered.

"No, it isn't!" I said with disgust. "Santa lives at the North Pole. It's the Hermit."

Except for the snow-white hair, the full white beard, the chubby red face, and the big round belly, the old man didn't look at all like Santa Claus.

The Hermit had with him a medium-sized dog of the lower-class variety. He was a friendly dog, however. As soon as we stepped out of the bushes, he came running and bounced high into the air all around us.

The old man looked us over and then gave us a crinkly smile, so we walked up to him.

"Are you the Hermit?" Pat asked. He knew next to nothing about manners.

The old man chuckled and looked down at his reflection in the water.

"I guess I am," he said. "And where did you fellows sprout from?"

"Our father bought this farm," I answered.

At that very moment, a fish interrupted us. Pat and I watched openmouthed while the old man patiently reeled it in.

"What kind of fish is it?" I asked him, after it had been landed.

"A supper fish," he said.

Meanwhile, the dog had begun to bounce again.

"What's his name?" Pat asked as the animal ascended into the air.

"Don't rightly know. Reckon I'd call him Bounce if he

were mine," the Hermit replied as the beast returned to the earth.

"Isn't he yours?" I asked as the animal went up again.

"Nope, he's not mine," he said. "Came wanderin' in here last week. You want him?"

Of course we wanted him. We always wanted dogs—all dogs, any dogs. But the Sergeant had given us very clear instructions.

"Our father says we can't have a dog yet," I glumly informed him. "He's waiting until we can get a purebred German shepherd."

Meanwhile, the particular animal in question had slowly dribbled his way down to the ground and was now engaged in sniffing over my brother.

When the old man headed upstream with his fish, we followed closely on his heels, and the dog bounced happily along after us.

"I wish we could take him home," Pat sighed as he attempted to pet him on his way up.

"Me too," I agreed.

"There's my place," the Hermit announced. "It ain't much."

Ahead of us, in a pretty little clearing next to the stream, sat an old shack with a rusty stovepipe sticking crookedly out of its roof. To the right of it, off in the bush, there was a wooden outhouse of the same make and model number as our own. All in all, I thought it was a very attractive neighborhood in which to live.

"There's nothing fancy in here," he warned us, as he

led the way into his gray-board shack. "Maybe a biscuit and a cup of tea."

The inside of his home was warm and cozy. There was one room and one window, neither of which had been spoiled by overcleaning. There was also some furniture. There was a cot, a washstand, a table with a coal-oil lamp, and a chair with wooden arms and a leather cushion. A huge, black kitchen stove murmured contentedly at the far end of the room, and I saw there were several shelves of books on the wall above the cot. Against the little wall space remaining, eight wooden butter boxes were stacked up with the open ends out. These were crammed with just about everything in the world. I decided that I would be very content to live in a convenient, well-equipped place like this.

Following the directions contained in the flicking of his hand, Pat and I sat down politely on his cot while he prepared our snack. Bounce immediately squirmed in between us and licked up at our faces with such enthusiasm that we were obliged to push him back to the floor.

"He likes you, that dog," the Hermit observed. "You ought to take him with you when you go."

"Our father wouldn't let us keep him," I reminded the old man.

"Oh yeah," he laughed. "I plumb forgot. He's saving up for a purebred German shepherd."

On hearing this, the unwanted dog lay down by the stove with his uncertified head between his paws, staring sadly up at us with apologetic brown eyes.

When the tea was finally ready, we found there was

not—as I feared there might be—any shortage of sugar. We borrowed his spoon and got the sugar directly from a big can under the table.

While we scooped a small truckload of sugar into our tea, he was busy pouring something else into his. Whatever it was, it came out of a whiskey bottle. When this was done, he tasted his concoction and contentedly wiped his jaw with his arm. Then he settled down in his chair and lit a pipe. Through the haze of blue smoke that soon surrounded us, Pat and I watched his every move while we gnawed like little rats at our rocklike biscuits. I'd never in my life found any article of food I couldn't bite into, but on that occasion it was a near thing.

Over by the stove the commonplace dog relentlessly ground up and swallowed down all the biscuits that the old man rolled across the floor to him.

"Thirty years I spent in the desert," the Hermit said suddenly. "Thirty years! Before, during, and after the war."

"Our father was in the war," I informed him.

"I don't mean that little war!" he laughed. "I mean the big war. The Great War!"

I didn't know anything about the Great War, except that my grandfather had been killed in it. I took a sip of tea and said nothing further.

"Yup! Yessir! Them were the days, all right! Many's the time me and Larry nearly died of thirst out there on the Sinai. Thank God for the Arabs, or I wouldn't be here at all. Yes, boys, it was hard! It was tough! But we loved every minute of it!"

"What's an Arab?" Pat asked.

"You never heard of Arabs?" He squinted at Pat in disbelief.

"I have!" I said. And I did, in fact, know quite a lot about Arabs—about how they frequently traveled to and fro on magic carpets and drank olive oil for breakfast.

"Yup!" he went on. "Many's the time the desert Bedouin saved our skins. Me and Larry's. But you had to get the right ones to save you, or you were really done for."

"What happened if they were the wrong ones?" I asked.

He looked at me and smiled, then drew his finger across his throat.

At this point the Hermit stood up and began to root in an old sea chest that I hadn't noticed until then. After a time, he came up with something that turned out to be a picture album. And when he sat down between us and opened the leather door of the album, all the things of his past—the desert, the camels, the palm trees, the tents, the Arabs, and, especially, his friend Larry—got up from nothing and began to float around in front of us.

"And here," he said, "is Larry and me out on patrol, and we're lost. We know we're somewhere in the Middle East and that's about it. My canteen is empty now, and Larry's drunk all his water too. See? Here we are, dying of thirst. That's me there under the umbrella, and that's Larry in the sun helmet. And it's Ben Hassad, our guide, who's taking the picture. He ain't got a clue where we are, and he's dying right along with us."

The old hermit chuckled away to himself, no doubt remembering how much fun it had been out there dying of thirst on the desert with Larry. Then he turned another page, and his finger went into another picture.

"That's my camel Sheila lying down behind me. She were the darnedest camel I ever had. Hard to get up and a man-biter if there ever was one. Larry used to say that if I ever learned to handle Sheila, then I might be able to manage a wife. But I never did."

"What happened to her?" I asked.

"Sheila? Oh, we ate her once when we was lost in the desert. . . . Now, Larry, there was a man who knew camels. That's why the Arabs thought so highly of him."

When we arrived at the end of the picture album, I felt like I'd been on a long journey through old Arabia. But then I saw the brass alarm clock on the table said four o'clock, and if the argument back home was over, they might be wondering where Pat and I had gone to eat our lunch. So we thanked the old hermit for the tea and went outside to head home.

Bounce was intent on coming with us. As soon as we started off, he barked joyously and bounded happily along-side us, and he absolutely refused to respond to the old hermit's call. In the end it was necessary to haul him back and shut him inside the shack so that we could leave the place without him.

While we were walking home, I saw a large cloud of dust moving around on our northwest quarter.

"What is it?" Pat asked.

"It's him on the tractor," I said.

"What's he doing?" Pat asked. He knew nothing at all about farming.

"He's planting summer fallow," I said with an air of superiority.

As we approached the house, Mother came out to greet us.

"Don't tell her about the Hermit," I said instinctively.

"Where've you been?" she asked us.

"I don't know," Pat said with a blank look. He was never a very resourceful liar.

"We were down by the creek," I hastened to inform her.

"I know exactly where you've been," she said, shaking her head at me.

"We saw the old hermit," I instantly confessed. My greatest gift was that I always knew when it was time to throw in the towel.

"You shouldn't have gone there," she said with a frown. "Your father said not to."

We hung our heads in shame.

"So, don't tell him," she warned, which was exactly what I was planning not to do in the first place.

An hour or so later, the Sergeant returned from the field for supper. We watched him come into the kitchen and go straight to the washstand without a glance at any of us. Just from the way he walked, I knew we were in trouble. A moment later, when he'd finished washing and had begun to comb his hair, he looked deep into the mirror that hung on the wall over the washbasin.

"You two went to see that old man, didn't you?" he asked.

I was prepared to allow Pat to answer, but Pat looked up his sleeve and said nothing.

"They're children. They're curious," Mother said.

"I told them not to," he said in a low voice, turning to look directly at us.

"Well, perhaps they shouldn't have, but you know how kids are."

"That's it!" the Sergeant exclaimed. "That-is-it! Now he goes for sure!"

"But . . ."

Poor Mother didn't get to finish her sentence, because the big sergeant was already gone. We went outside and watched him disappear into the woods, headed in the direction of the southeast pasture.

"Where's he going?" Pat asked. As usual, events had completely outdistanced him.

"To tell the old hermit to move," Mother said with a frown.

"Why does he want him to move?" I asked.

"I don't know. Come in and get your supper," she said with a sigh.

Just before sunset, she came outside and sat down on the steps. When Pat and I came over, we saw that there was a worried look in her eyes.

"Your father should have been home hours ago," she said. "When you were there, did you notice if the Hermit had a gun?"

But even as she asked the question, we saw him emerge from the woods and come toward us. Not straight toward us, but toward us in an exploratory way—in the manner of a confused snake.

Something suddenly emerged from the woods behind him, and shouts of joy erupted from Pat and me. The Sergeant had not come home alone. Bounce was with him.

As soon as our new dog arrived at the steps, he bounded joyously all over the place, pausing only long enough to lick our faces. But the Sergeant wasn't bounding. In fact, he walked with a noticeable slant, and there was a silly smile on his face. There was also a glazed look in his eyes, and I saw Mother frown as he tilted around and lurched toward her.

"Well, did you evict the squatter?" she asked in a voice so dry it could have killed grass.

"Couldn't!" The Sergeant laughed. "Turned out he's a veteran like me. From the Great War, though."

"Oh, I see," she said, pursing her lips at him.

"Hey, look what I brought home!" the Sergeant exclaimed. "He gave me to it . . . it me . . . me it. What? Guess? A dog! Where are you, doggy?"

At that particular moment Bounce was high in the air over Pat, and the Sergeant couldn't locate him.

"I see it's a purebred German shepherd," Mother said in that same bone-dry voice.

"I think there's some shepherd in him. There's got to be! There's everything else!" The Sergeant continued to laugh.

"No doubt," Mother said.

"You know," the Sergeant went on, "I think the old fellow actually knew Lawrence of Arabia. Spent years and years out there on the desert. Showed me all his pictures. Many's the time he and Larry nearly died of thirst!"

"Well, he's making up for it now," Mother said, still frowning. "Come inside and I'll fix you some coffee."

"And guess what?" the Sergeant asked as he groped his way up the steps.

"I can't imagine," Mother replied.

"The old buzzard looks just like Santa Claus," he said.

CHAPTER FOUR
Charlie Pears

Bounce was a wonderful dog. Pat and I were very happy that we got him. However, he was not the smartest dog in the world. He liked to fetch sticks, and we spent a lot of time throwing them around the place for him to fetch. The only trouble was that he often forgot what the stick we threw looked like, and he would bring back a substitute— the bigger the better. Sometimes he would drag an entire log out of the woods and look up at us expectantly, waiting for us to throw it back. He also seemed to think that Cannibal was a dog, and he liked to chase him around and smell him, even though Cannibal had a tendency to hiss at him.

In spite of his shortcomings, we all loved Bounce. However, one dog doesn't make up for losing an entire way of life and being forced to live out in the middle of nowhere and having to haul water from the well all day long. I still hated it, and I still hated the Sergeant for ruining my life.

As for Pat, he'd spotted some wild ducks down by Schneider's slough, and he was happy. He spent hours standing at the edge of the water, watching them glide around like a bunch of little Mississippi paddle wheelers.

One day, when Pat and I were visiting the slough, the Sergeant walked up the road and looked at them. He shook his head.

"They're just mud hens," he said.

"They aren't chickens—they're ducks," Pat countered. He thought he knew a duck when he saw one. I agreed with him for once. They sure looked like ducks to me.

"No, they aren't chickens," the Sergeant conceded. "They're ducks. But they're a very poor kind of duck. No good for eating," he explained.

The thought that anyone would eat a duck had evidently never occurred to my brother, and he was horrified. He was so upset that he wouldn't eat his supper until they promised him we'd never try to eat a duck.

Sometimes at night, through the transom in the floor, we could hear them talking across the kitchen table while they drank their coffee. They were always talking about money and always wondering how they were going to get enough for the next payment on the mortgage on the farm. One night they talked about how the bank might take the farm away from them if they missed another payment. I thereupon fell to my knees and prayed to God that they would miss the payment and that the bank would do its duty. Then we'd all move back to Wistola and live happily ever after.

"What are you doing?" Pat asked me.

"I'm praying," I said.

Pat thereupon fell to his knees and began to pray beside me.

"What are you praying for?" I asked suspiciously.

"I'm praying that Mother will get the ducks on Saturday," he said.

For several days now, the Sergeant had been puttering around with one of the old buildings. First he patched the building up and put an old window in it, then he built a sturdy corral fence all around it, using logs he made from some lodgepole pine trees he took from the woods. The next day, after lunch, he announced that he was going to get some pigs. Pat eagerly climbed into Maggie to go with him, but not me.

At the last minute, leaning out of Maggie's window, he asked me if I wanted to come with them, but I refused. I didn't like being in the truck with him. I didn't even like being around him. He was always trying to teach me things I wasn't interested in, such as the difference between pine and spruce trees, and the proper way to use a hammer, and how to saw a piece of wood in two, and how to join one piece of wood to another. I hated it all. I hated everything about the country. I even hated his wood.

They came home with the pigs and let them loose in the pigpen. Pat was overjoyed. He liked all animals, whereas I liked only certain animals, and pigs were not on my list. I thought they were ugly and dirty. But before I knew what had happened, I found that I was in charge of them. First the Sergeant showed me how to make pig mash out of oats and corn and vegetables, mixed in with table scraps and everything else we wanted to get rid of. Then he showed me how to deliver it to the pig trough.

From that time forward, every morning after breakfast and every evening after supper, I had to make their mash and fill their trough with it. I didn't blame the pigs, however, and I gave them plenty to eat. They also found food by themselves by rooting around in the ground.

In time, I found that I didn't dislike them as much as I had in the beginning. There was one middle-sized one that seemed smarter than the others, and he seemed to like me. I named him Peter, and I began to talk to him at feeding time.

When the Sergeant heard me talking to him and calling him by his name, he came over and shook his head at me.

"They aren't pets," he said. "Just feed them and leave them alone. When they get big enough, we'll be butchering them."

And there I was. My only friend in the whole world was a pig, and eventually I was going to have to eat him. It was a sad thing. But I knew the Sergeant was right, and I stopped trying to make friends among the pigs.

About a week after the pigs arrived, Mother bought two white ducks, and Pat was very happy. So were the ducks. They headed for the pond as soon as they were let loose. Pat was the one who fed them, and whenever he went outside they came running up from the pond.

A few days after the ducks came to live with us, the Sergeant bought a cow from a farmer named Elmer, who lived down the road a couple of miles past the Schneiders. The cow's name was Goldie. I then discovered that cows have to be milked every day, when they're in season. This was Mother's job, but she taught me how to do it, and then it became my job too—whenever she was too busy to do it and I was within shouting distance. Pat missed out on all this because his hands were too small.

I didn't actually mind the milking. I liked Goldie. She had large, sad eyes. She seemed to understand my unhappiness and somehow to share it.

As I milked her I often thought about my new life in California. I wondered what would actually happen to me when I got there. I dreamed that I'd be living in a big house, like the ones I'd seen in the movies. I knew that the ocean was right there in front of Hollywood, and I imagined I was swimming in it. I knew how to swim very well.

That's one of the great things we did in the summer when we lived in Wistola. Swimming. After lunch, whenever we didn't go to the movies, we'd head for the Rotary Park. With the hot sun burning above us, we'd swim and float in the cool water of the pool all afternoon, until suppertime. Pat and Milton, Sherry and Bobby—and me.

Pat could swim like a fish, though he was only six. He also jumped off the high diving board, even though Mother had forbidden it. But she wasn't there to stop him, and I didn't want to spoil his fun.

Along with an abundance of milk, Goldie provided a lot of cream, which Mother used in all her baking. After Goldie's arrival, Mother's homemade bread got better and the buns got fatter and more luscious. And now there was always lots of butter on the table. There was no doubt about it. The food in the country was better. I had to admit it.

One warm afternoon late in July, I found Mother standing on a chair in the living room. She was putting up the new curtains she'd made on her Singer sewing machine. I threw myself into an easy chair and emitted a huge sigh.

"I wish we still lived in Wistola," I muttered. "There's nothing to do out here."

"I would seriously advise you not to say that when your father's around," she responded.

I understood her meaning and immediately went back to my usual complaint.

"I miss Milton. I miss Bobby and Sherry," I moaned.

"Well, don't worry," she answered. "You'll soon make all kinds of new friends. You'll see. There's lots of kids out here."

"Then where are they?" I responded with a gargantuan whine.

Suddenly a very formidable voice descended on me from the doorway. It was the Sergeant's voice.

"Stop that whining!" he roared.

"Stop shouting!" Mother exclaimed. "You almost made me fall off the chair!"

As for me, I jumped a foot straight up in the air. When I came back down, I gazed up at him with clouded eyes. I was still afraid of him, especially when he was angry.

"If you really want some friends," he said impatiently, glowering down at me, "then get up off your duff and go down the road and knock on a few doors, and you'll find more friends than you can shake a stick at!"

After he'd gone outside and I could think again, it occurred to me that what he was suggesting wasn't really such a bad idea. Go down the road and find a friend. I could do that.

I hadn't even reached the dirt road out front when Pat came running and shouting after me.

"Are you going to look at the other ducks?" he inquired.

"No, I hate those ducks, I'm going down the road to find a friend," I informed him.

"Can I come too?" he asked.

"Okay," I said. "But don't bother my friend when I find him."

We stood at the front of our lane for a moment, while I tried to decide which way to go. I could see Mr. Schneider's white farmhouse in the distance on my right, on the other side of the slough, but all the Schneider children were girls. There were five of them all together, and I'd already discovered that playing with more than one girl at a time is disturbing to the brain.

"We'll go that way," I said, turning left and marching toward the west hill, away from the cluster of Schneider girls.

When we got to the top of the hill, I could see a small, yellow saltbox house. It had probably been a nice little place once upon a time, but now it was more like a badly run-down shack. But it was something, at least, and I couldn't see anything else close by.

"We'll try in there," I said.

The front yard was littered with junk—a bedspring, a decaying icebox, an old stove, piles of rotten boards, wagon wheels, rusty pieces of machinery, abandoned vehicles from ancient times, and many other things I couldn't identify. A jungle of high weeds was growing all through this junk-filled area and all around it.

As I looked over the scene, I saw a trail around one side of the junkyard. It led from the road up to the house, but it was much more interesting for us to try to make our way through the junk-filled obstacle course right in front of us.

"We could play in here if we find a friend in that house," I suggested as we crawled through the cab of an old, doorless Model T truck and then went under an ancient iron-wheeled tractor.

As we left the junkyard behind and approached the

front of the house, I noticed something that made me freeze on the spot. The ground all around was littered with beer bottles. I stared at them, and my old Wistola instincts welled up in me. If only Milton could see this, I thought.

"Look at all the beer bottles," Pat said.

"Don't touch them," I ordered. "They might think we're trying to steal them."

But maybe, just maybe, they were not aware of their value. So maybe they would give them to me. And now that Mother was taking us to Wistola on Saturdays, I would be able to cash them in. Money!

I was thinking all this and still looking at all the beer bottles, a huge fortune just lying on the ground, when I suddenly remembered why I was there. I was there to find a friend.

On closer examination, however, it didn't look to me as if there was likely to be a friend inside that house. It looked as if it had been abandoned for years and years. The roof was sagging, the chimney top was gone, and the old yellow paint was peeling off everywhere. What's worse, the two front windows were covered over with boards, and there were even boards across the front door. And then I noticed that bales of rotten straw had been thrown all around the bottom of the house to help cover the holes in the crumbling foundation.

In short, the place didn't seem very promising.

"We'll go around the back and take a look," I said, leading the way.

We had just come around to the side of the house

when, right in front of us, a beer bottle came flying out through an open window. It sailed right across the dirt trail and landed in the pasture on the other side of the barbed-wire fence.

"There's somebody in there," Pat observed.

In the meantime, while Pat's eye had been fastened on the window, my eye had been following the flight of the beer bottle. I ran over to the fence and looked on the other side of it. The pasture was littered with beer bottles. Thousands of them. A fortune!

I went back to the house and stood to one side of the window.

"Hello?" I said. "We're out here. It's my brother and me."

"Who are ya?" a husky voice grunted from inside.

"We live down the road," I informed it.

"Come in and let me see ya," the voice ordered.

"Can we come in through the window?" Pat asked.

"Come in through the back door," the voice said.

Around the back we paused briefly to look at a battered old Ford truck, then we went onto the sagging porch and up to the screen door. I opened it tentatively and peered inside.

I saw a large kitchen room with a worn and dirty linoleum floor. I saw a big wooden table all cluttered up with used dishes. Near some nondescript cupboards that had no doors was a counter heaped up with more dirty dishes. The dingy walls were of a decaying yellow color, just like the outside, but I saw there was a nice picture of the Sacred Heart of Jesus nailed to one of the window frames.

There were some wooden chairs by the table, and on the far side of the room, there was an old living room easy chair with an open case of beer on one side of it and a chamber pot on the other. In between these two things, reclining on the easy chair with his feet up on a lard box and a bottle of beer in his hand, was a stocky young man with black hair and a chubby face. He was naked from the waist up, and his massive chest was thoroughly matted with curly black hair. The man had clearly not shaved for quite a while, and black whiskers poked their way through the skin of his face.

The burly man sat as immobile as a giant toad and stared at us without smiling. But he did not really look unfriendly. He looked about neutral. He grunted and motioned with the beer bottle for us to come the rest of the way in, then raised the bottle to his lips and drank fully from it, staring at us all the while.

I looked around some more and saw a scruffy orange cat reclining on an old wooden bench behind me. Above the bench there was a row of spikes in the wall, from which an entire wardrobe of badly soiled clothes was hanging. The coveralls nearest me were a particularly sad item, heavily stained with grease and oil and caked at the knees with a mixture of mud and cow dung. The big hobnailed boots under the bench were badly scuffed and the soles and heels were worn. I saw at a glance that they'd never met a shoe brush going in the opposite direction, and I immediately contrasted them with the Sergeant's clean army boots, which he shone to a high gleam every Saturday morning.

The man leaned over and spit directly down into the chamber pot with easy aplomb, and I saw he was chewing a gob of tobacco.

"Who are ya?" he asked us.

"We live down there," Pat said, pointing at the east window.

"Yer people bought the Smith place," he said. "I heard about ya. What's yer names?"

I told him our names, and he grunted at us in acknowledgment.

"What's yours?" I asked.

"Charlie Pears," he replied.

He then hiked his bottle to his mouth and tilted his head back to drain it. I was growing uncomfortable, especially when he stood up and walked toward us. But he stopped when he was about halfway across the room and, with a quick wrench of his arm, sailed the bottle clear through the far window. I took this as a sign we could relax.

"Do you want your empty beer bottles?" I asked boldly.

"Nah. Ya can have 'em," he said without any hesitation.

I was rich! Unbelievably rich! I smiled broadly and was about to thank him when he spoke again.

"Ya got any sisters?" he asked.

"No," I said.

"This here place needs a woman's sweet hand," he explained as he settled back in his easy chair and plopped his feet up on the box.

I looked around again, and I couldn't bring myself to disagree with him.

"Ah don't want no prettifying woman," he said. "Ah want a good Christian workin' woman who don't take to fancy-dancing around and all that prettifying stuff."

I nodded my head in solemn agreement.

"Yup!" he said concussively, crossing his hands over his protruding belly. "Charlie Pears ain't gonna get himself tied up with no prettifying woman. No siree!"

After I'd wandered around for a few minutes, I spotted something that interested me greatly—a long-barreled shotgun standing in the corner. Pat saw it too, and a second later, we were down on our knees next to it, admiring the intricate design on the highly polished stock, as well as the bright silver embossing on the side of the chamber and the long, gleaming blue-black barrel.

"Can we touch your gun?" I asked.

"Help yerself," he grunted.

Within a few minutes Pat and I had advanced ourselves to the point where we were exercising the gun at the window, pretending to shoot at imaginary bandits who were trying to get at our beer bottles out on the pasture.

"Bang . . . bang," I said quietly, and there was an answering burp from across the room. I looked behind and saw that his eyelids were down, so I put the gun back through the window and returned to my war with the bandits. And then, in order to achieve a greater degree of realism, I cocked the hammer and pulled the trigger.

The blast that followed deafened me instantly, and the recoil sent me careening backward across the room until I finally came down on my backside, right at Charlie's feet.

I looked up at him, expecting the worst.

"It were loaded," he said with a grin.

After some time had gone by, and after an in-depth discussion about how nice and helpful a good workin' woman would be, we got to know Charlie and he got to know us and we felt quite at home there. "Help yerselves" seemed to be his general approach to things. So much so that we felt able to leave him alone and were soon running around outside, busy mining the one great natural resource the place had in abundance. Beer bottles. Some were broken, but most were not. Within a few minutes, Pat and I had collected a great pile of them, which we stashed at the southeast end of the junkyard, safe there until transportation out could be arranged.

"When Mother takes us into Wistola, we can come up here and get a load to take in with us, and we'll have lots and lots of money to spend!" I said excitedly as I surveyed my vast new fortune.

I could not remember ever having been so happy, and I was simply overwhelmed with gratitude toward my new friend, Charlie. So much so that I went back to thank him again. And while on the way up there, it occurred to me that not only had I acquired a fortune today, but also, judging from the look of things, I had discovered an unending supply of continued wealth.

"Can we come in again?" I asked through the screen door.

Charlie waved us in. He was standing with his orange cat in his arms, surveying a mess of undone laundry that lay piled up in one corner.

"Ah really needs to marry me a workin' woman," he solemnly declared.

He set the cat down on the floor and continued to stare morosely at the laundry pile.

"I got to scrub all them clothes myself," he muttered.

"Thanks for the beer bottles," I said.

He nodded, then turned and went over to the line of spikes by the door, where he selected a large checkered shirt to cover his top half with. Then he sat down on the bench to put his big boots on, while the cat leaped up beside him and continuously rubbed its head against his thick right arm.

"Got ta go check the cattle," Charlie grunted. "Ain't been out there for a week."

We followed him out to the porch, but then he abruptly turned to the left and walked over to the far end of it, where he did a strange thing.

"He's peeing," Pat whispered to me.

He certainly was. I looked at the outhouse straight in front of me and then at Charlie at the end of the porch. The Sergeant would not approve of this, I thought.

"Had to take a leak." Charlie grinned when he turned around.

When he got into the truck, he paused for a moment, then bent forward to start it up.

"Can we come with you?" Pat asked, looking up at him.

"Sure. Hop in," he grunted.

There was a very foul odor loose in Charlie's truck, a mixture of fresh beer fumes and certain other noxious stenches, mixed in with the smells that over the years had sunk into the upholstery. I attempted to roll my window down, but it didn't work, so I just sat there and stared bleakly at the insect collection on the windshield while I tried not to breathe very much.

"Where are we going?" Pat asked after we'd bumped out of the farmyard and gone over an old Texas gate into the pasture.

"Got ta take a look at my cows," he said. "Got ta see how the calfies is coming along."

We bumped merrily along, and I was quite enjoying the ride now that I'd adjusted to the truck's odor. Then, suddenly, the land we were driving on disappeared. At first I thought we were falling off a cliff, but we weren't. We had just come to the edge of a big hill and were now going down it in sideways fashion. I grabbed the dash and hung on to it for dear life, and Pat did likewise.

"Is it going to fall over?" I asked nervously, since we were at that moment approaching ninety degrees off the horizontal.

"Heck, no!" Charlie laughed. "I go down here all the time!"

He was right. The bottom of the hill was now in sight,

and it looked like we were going to live after all. But then Charlie wrenched the wheel around and the truck abruptly turned and we began a vertical nosedive straight down the rest of the hill. For a split second just then, I wondered if perhaps he had decided to commit suicide and was taking us along for company.

"Hold on, boys!" Charlie squawked. "Need some extra speed to make it up the next hill."

He was referring to the cliff that began just a few yards beyond where the steep hill we were coming down ended. I could see that we would need speed to make it up that next one. And soon we would need wings and a harp, too.

"Are we going to get killed?" I asked, hanging frantically on to the dashboard.

But Charlie only laughed. We then hit the bottom of the hill with a *whump* that drove me a foot down into the seat.

"Up she goes!" he squealed.

We were now going straight up, it seemed to me, for gravity was pressing my head against the back of the seat and all I could see through the windshield was vertical blue sky.

"Hold on, boys!" Charlie shouted as we approached the top. "The next one is the bad one!"

I closed my eyes and began to pray.

When at last the truck stopped, I threw myself out and bent over the swirling ground. And I wasn't a moment too soon. Had I stayed in that truck for one more second, I would have completely ruined Charlie's upholstery.

Upon completing my last retch, I closed my mouth and sat down on the ground.

"What's the matter, kid?" Charlie asked. "Are ya sick or something?"

"I'm okay," I said, gazing up at him with all the sprightliness of a smoked mackerel.

"That was fun!" Pat exclaimed happily.

Charlie laughed at him and waved at us to follow him to the nearby poplar bush.

"They's usually somewhere around here," he said as he peered into the trees. "You guys go down that way and see if ya can scare up anything."

And so while Charlie went straight ahead into the trees, Pat and I went down to the end of the bush, where a large animal came around the corner and looked at us. It had horns, and there was little sign of intelligence in its eyes.

"Is it a bull?" Pat asked.

"Don't be stupid," I said. "It's got udders just like Goldie's. It's only a dumb cow."

"What are we supposed to do?" Pat asked as we looked at the cow and the cow looked at us.

"I guess we should tell Charlie," I replied. I then raised my hands to form a shouting cup around my mouth.

"WE FOUND ONE!" I screamed in Charlie's direction.

It then became evident that the cow—or whatever it was—did not like the sound of my voice, for it tossed its head and snorted at me.

"We'd better get out of here," I suggested quietly.

We turned and began to run, and we did so not a moment too soon, for the beast was after us.

"Run faster!" I screamed at Pat behind me, having an eye to later difficulties back home should the cow manage to catch up and dismantle him.

"I can't run any faster!" he screamed back.

But then the cow stopped. And I stopped too, after a few more steps. Pat, however, kept on going all the way back to the truck.

"See!" I yelled at him with a mixture of contempt and triumph. "It's afraid of me! It's only a stupid old cow. Shoo! Shoo, you old cow! Get out of here! Git!"

I then waved my arms at it, and a second later, it came after me again. And this time it nearly got a horn into me via the back door. In truth, I barely managed to hurl myself under the truck in the nick of time. And there I waited, next to Pat, for what seemed like forever, while the beast stood nearby and flared its nostrils at us.

When Charlie finally came back from the woods, the cow ran off.

"They's all here," he said. "Let's go!"

I crawled out from under the truck and climbed inside. It didn't smell so bad to me now.

"That cow tried to kill me," I informed him.

Charlie laughed. "Yeah, I seen it," he said as he started up the truck. "I'll tell you what. Next time a cow starts to chase ya, just turn around and punch it on the nose. That always stops them."

"Punch the cow?" I said with disbelief. "Are you kidding?"

"No, I ain't kidding," he solemnly declared. "That's why they call them cowboy fellers cowpunchers."

After chuckling to himself for a minute, he stepped on the clutch and shifted the truck into gear.

"Can we go back a different way?" I asked him.

"Sure, kid," he said. "Which way you want to go?"

"The level way," I replied.

"Sorry, kid." Charlie laughed. "There ain't no level way."

When we got back to the shack, I followed Charlie and Pat inside—as soon as I was finished retching. After we were finished looking at the shotgun again, Pat and I sat down on the bench. We both began to pet the orange cat, which at once began to purr like an outboard motor. Meanwhile, Charlie shook one of his pots out and dumped two cans of wieners and beans into it. This he transported over to the Primus stove, and after a few adjustments, followed by an explosive *whoosh* of flame when he held a match to it, things started cooking. Then he seemed to remember us.

"You guys want some grub?" he asked.

"What time is it?" I asked back.

"It's gittin' on to four-thirty," he said, after briefly consulting his pocket watch.

"Okay, we can stay and eat," I said. Our own supper wasn't until six, so there was no need to rush off.

Charlie dumped a third can of wieners and beans into the pot, then he sat down in his chair and crossed his legs. The orange cat promptly ran across the room and perched itself on his foot. He began to gently lift it up and down in the air.

"Darn cat," Charlie muttered.

Later he stood up and looked into the pot and gave the contents another stir.

"Go get yer plates," he said. "And bring one for me."

I couldn't find where he kept his clean plates, and then I discovered the reason why. There weren't any.

"Just wipe some off with that dishpan rag," he instructed me as he stirred the pot.

As soon as I had cleaned up the required number of plates, I brought them to him on the run, for my appetite was up.

"No, no," he grunted. "Ya gotta have bread under. Go git it. It's over there."

When I returned, he ladled the beans and wieners onto the bread and we cleared away our places at the table and dug in.

"It's good!" Pat exclaimed.

"Ain't you guys never had beans and wienies before?" he asked us.

"I don't think so," I admitted.

He looked at us with an amazed expression.

"Don't yer mother know how to cook?"

That got no response from us. We had no wish to undermine our mother just because she wasn't as good a cook as he was.

"Where's your mother?" Pat asked after a while.

"Mum's buried out there," he said, gesturing to the

north with the heel of his bottle. He swept a spoonful of beans into his mouth and grunted. "Never knew her. She went under when I was borned."

"Oh," we said.

"T'were my paw that raised me up to be a man," he went on. "As best he could."

"Where's he?" I asked.

"He's buried out there too," he said with a nod of his head. "With Mum."

When we could eat no more, Pat and I stood up to go. We felt it was time.

"I'll give you fellers a ride down," he said. "Gonna go into town and look around."

On the way down the hill, he glanced over at me.

"I'm particular lookin' fer a widow-woman," he said. "'Cause they know how to wash clothes proper, and they ain't gonna be so prettifying with all that fancy-dancing around and stuff."

I agreed wholeheartedly with his philosophy of women, and I told him so.

The Sergeant was drinking a cup of coffee and Mother was at the stove stirring her soup when we came in. They looked at us expectantly.

"Well, did you find a friend?" he asked.

"Yes, we did!" Pat and I responded enthusiastically.

"What's his name?" Mother asked.

"His name is Charlie," Pat reported.

"He's a really great guy!" I added.

"Well, isn't that nice!" Mother chirped.

"Didn't I tell you?" the Sergeant said with a smug smile. "All you had to do was go out and knock on a few doors."

"And guess what?" I said excitedly.

"What?" the Sergeant responded.

"He's going to give us all his empty beer bottles," I announced.

"And he pees right off the end of his porch!" Pat proclaimed.

Shortly afterward, we were instructed not to visit Charlie too often, because he was too old to be our daily friend.

"They don't like him," Pat said later on, when we were up in the loft lying on the hay.

"It's because he drinks beer," I said.

"What does beer taste like?" he asked.

"It's awful," I said.

"Are you going to find another friend?" Pat asked me.

"No," I said. "I'm sick of finding friends."

Anyway, what was the use of making new friends out here when I would soon be living in California?

CHAPTER FIVE
The Big Tree

"Let's go climb the big tree," Pat said one morning after we'd hauled two loads of bottles down from Charlie's.

The tree he was referring to was an ancient poplar, as tall as a three-story building in Wistola, with immense arms that reached out in every direction. It was the giant of all the trees in the woods at the back of the farmstead.

"Not again!" I frowned. "That's kid stuff! Can't you think of anything else?"

"Like what?" he asked.

From the top of the big tree, the old farmhouse down below us looked like a matchbox, and I could see the mountains in the west and all the rolling green countryside for miles around. I even imagined I could see Wistola. I couldn't, of course, because it was too far away. But I told Pat I could.

"Where? I can't see it," he complained.

"You need glasses," I said with a scornful smile. It was always enjoyable to take advantage of his youth and ignorance. On this particular occasion, however, my enjoyment was interrupted when Pat squinted at the horizon and nodded.

"Yeah, I see it," he said.

"Where?" I asked.

He tried to show me where it was, but try as I might, I could not see it. Eventually I began to wonder if he was really seeing it.

Later, while I was hanging upside down from the highest branch capable of supporting my weight, I saw a familiar figure come out of the house and head toward the chicken coop with a bowl of feed.

"Quiet," I whispered. "There goes Mother."

Mother did not approve of our climbing to the top of the big tree. In fact, she was generally opposed to any kind of fun that put our lives at risk. Fortunately, however, we were well hidden by the tree leaves.

Some time after Mother had come and gone, I began to grow weary. Not weary of the tree, for once you get up there, great height is a glorious thing. However, despite rumors to the contrary, man was never intended to perch in trees for any length of time. After a while the rounded tree limbs began to wear away the skin, then your sitting bones grew painfully weary, and then some of the lower muscles began to urgently complain about their unaccustomed stretching.

As we started down the tree, we paused to take a final look around.

"I wish our house was up here," Pat sighed.

"Don't be crazy. You couldn't get a house up here," I scoffed.

"Well, Tarzan's house is in a tree," he protested.

That was true. I had to admit it, having seen it myself at the Roxy Theater in Wistola.

Suddenly I was so overwhelmed with excitement that I nearly fell off the tree. For at that instant a truly wonderful idea had come out of nowhere and occupied my head. We could build a house right here in this tree!

But first I had to check on one thing. I quietly moved a branch aside and squinted at the southern horizon. Yes, the Sergeant was still out there, working the summer fallow with his old tractor.

In order to build a house, you need some boards. And some nails. And a few tools. Fortunately, we had an abundance of all three on the farm. However, the nails presented us with our first slight problem. The problem was not a lack of nails, but rather the opposite. There were altogether too many nails. There were two tin cans of brand-new nails and there were also seven cans full of used nails. These used nails were ones that the Sergeant had pulled out of old boards so that they could be used again. I really hesitated to use these old nails, the Sergeant having gone to all the trouble of pulling them out and making them straight again.

"Just take new ones," I warned Pat as we filled our pockets.

For our wood we chose select boards from a large pile behind the chicken coop. We then began to move them to the big tree. It was not easy. Work seldom is, unless you're a mattress tester. In any case, Pat and I set to work like a pair of Egyptian slaves, and we hauled enough wood to the base of the big tree to construct a fair-sized colonial mansion up there in the branches.

We were somewhat hampered in our activities, in our comings and goings from the wood stack, by the necessity of carrying out the hauling operation in a secretive manner. We wished to avoid the chance of being noticed by any sharp eyes that might happen to peer out through the kitchen window. In this regard, our dog was of no help at all. He insisted on bouncing up and down and all around the bushes, barking and doing everything in his power to attract Mother's attention. In the end it was necessary to quiet him down by putting the Seagram's purple bottle bag left over from Uncle Max's recent visit over his head. But even then the traitorous little mutt continued to bounce up and down like a live spring, and strange, muffled noises managed to make their way out of the bottle bag.

When at last all the materials were gathered at the construction site, the really slow part of the operation began: the hauling of the boards up the tree, one at a time. But Pat did the best he could, and I patiently held my temper in check while I waited for the next one to arrive. And the next. And the next. Slowly and steadily, Pat hauled them up and I nailed them in place, until finally we found we had constructed a fair-sized platform up there. It went out for some distance across two sturdy branches, high up in the top half of the tree. Then, by mutual agreement, we stopped working. I was getting tired, and Pat's eyes were beginning to glaze over. I think he was beginning to have negative thoughts, like the Hebrew slaves did before they fled from Egypt.

Of course it was not a complete house, but it was a complete floor, and we decided it was all we needed for the present. It was a good, solid platform too. No danger here. We jumped up and down all over it in order to make sure it wouldn't collapse on us.

"Look down there!" Pat exclaimed. "Bounce is trying to climb the tree!"

I looked down and saw that Pat wasn't kidding. Bounce had managed to get the bottle bag off his head and was making a determined effort to get up the tree. On one of his leaps, he nearly made it onto the first branch.

"Look out!" I shouted. "That isn't Bounce. It's an Amazon! She's attacking us!"

As we fought off the determined Amazon, throwing leaves and twigs down at her from our eagle's nest, we experienced true happiness.

After we'd defeated the Amazon attack, we felt totally safe. No one on earth could reach us up here. At least not without being spotted long before they arrived, for we could see everything in all directions for twenty miles. There was one thing I couldn't see, though. I couldn't see the tractor out in the field, where it was supposed to be.

"Where's Dad?" I asked.

"I'm right here," said a hard, low voice underneath us.

Pat and I both jumped, for it was quite a surprise to discover that the Sergeant was up there with us. We hardly believed our ears. However, when we bent over and looked under the platform, there he was, calmly squatting on the next branch down. Until that moment, I had not imagined that the Sergeant knew how to climb a tree.

"Hi, Dad!" Pat said.

I saw Bounce grinning up at me from the bottom of the tree. I could not understand why he had not signaled the Sergeant's approach. It was always his custom to bark at anything that moved.

A moment later, the Sergeant raised himself up to our level and looked down at us with hard eyes.

"We built it all by ourselves," Pat said with an air of restrained pride.

The Sergeant only glanced at him. Then, while holding on to an upper branch, he put one foot onto our platform and applied some weight. The board bent under the pressure, and he shook his head at us.

"Knock it down," he said.

We did what he told us to do, but sadly and reluctantly. And, a few moments later, our new home in the sky was nothing but a pile of old boards lying at the base of the tree. As we looked glumly around at the destruction, the

75

Sergeant reached down and took a board in his hand. He raised his leg high in the air and brought his foot crashing down on it. Under the impact of his heavy army boot, the board shattered into pieces.

"It's shiplap," he said. "It wasn't meant to take any real weight."

I looked at the broken board and I had to agree.

"And the nails you used weren't nearly long enough. And why did you use my new nails when I've got buckets and buckets of old ones?"

I could not explain. I could not even remember why, though I felt I'd had a reason at the time.

"You should have come to me first," he said in conclusion.

I nodded at him. It's difficult to disagree with hardened war veterans who are more than four times your size.

I cast my eyes sadly upward, to the top of the tree. Our house in the sky was gone, and I fully expected that he would punish us for building it without asking him first.

But then the Sergeant did something unexpected. He laughed and ruffled our hair with his big hands.

"Go get some of those big used nails from the seventh bucket and bring me a saw and bring over some of those heavy planks from behind the pigpen," he said. He looked down at us and smiled. "We're gonna rebuild it."

Actually, we didn't rebuild it. He did. The Sergeant did it all, while Pat and I hauled the planks up and provided murmurs of approval. I winced as I watched him drive the heavy nails through the thick planking into the poor branches. But now I saw clearly the difference between his method of construction and ours. He knew what he was doing.

"Okay," he said finally, "it's finished."

A second later, Pat and I were on the platform with him, and we could actually feel the difference. This platform was as solid as a log. There was absolutely no chance that these heavy planks would break.

"It's great!" I said enthusiastically.

"I even like it better than ours," Pat admitted.

Pat and I had only just begun to express our appreciation when, from far below, a very strange sound reached us. It was half like a muffled cry of despair and half like a scream. It was Mother. She was standing down on the path, looking up at us. Bounce was standing next to her, and it really looked like there was a grin on his face.

"Get down from there! Right now! Do you hear me?"

Then the Sergeant moved to the edge and smiled down at her.

"It's okay, Kathleen!" he shouted. "I'm up here with them!"

"You get down too, you big idiot!" Mother shouted back. "You'll all get killed!"

"No, we won't!" the Sergeant said with a laugh. "It's perfectly safe. I built it myself!"

"I don't care if Michelangelo built it! I want you all down here right this instant! Donald! Pat! You two get down here right now or you won't be going to town with me next Saturday! And I mean it!"

Going to Wistola on Saturday was the only thing I liked about living on the farm. As for Pat, he loved going to Wistola too. Two weeks ago, when we'd shot at a bird with our slingshots, Mother had gone to town without us, and the memory of that dismal Saturday was forever burned into our little brains. So we moaned and made grimaces of unhappiness, but Pat and I started down the tree.

We'd only come halfway down when the Sergeant leaned over the platform and shouted at us: "Just a minute, you two! Stay where you are!"

We were thus presented with a difficult situation, because we greatly respected the Sergeant. Not only had he cleaned the Nazis out of Europe, he also believed in corporal punishment. And we were the only corporals he had left.

"Get down here!" Mother shouted.

"Stay where you are!" the Sergeant ordered.

At this point we were halted about halfway down the big tree, pinned in place between these two great and opposed forces. We stayed there for a long moment, looking up and down with puzzled expressions, when the Sergeant suddenly erupted again.

"Don't be silly, Kathleen!" he shouted. "This thing's made of heavy planking! It's solid as a rock!"

And to prove his point, he began to jump up and down on the platform.

I doubt that the Sergeant would ever have swayed Mother to his point of view, even if he'd jumped up and down on it for ten years. As it happened, he didn't get a chance to even come close to that long. For when he came down on his fifth jump, there was a loud crack. Then one of the long supporting branches gave way, and one side of the platform suddenly tilted downward. Unfortunately, it was the side that the Sergeant happened to be jumping on.

He went off the platform just like a tree that has been cut down slowly topples over. It was almost a graceful thing, in fact, except for his hands clutching wildly at the air. And then he actually did manage to grab onto a branch with his hands. That branch might have saved him too, but it was not big enough. It was, in fact, a small twig. And, unfortunately, the Sergeant was a big man. Usually size is an advantage in life, but not when you're falling from a tree. The little twig snapped off in his hands as soon as it had determined how heavy he was.

The Sergeant was now headed straight down. He was still holding the twig when, just in front of Pat and me, he landed rearwise on another branch. Fortunately this was a big branch, and it did not break. It only bent down. Then it bent up again and the Sergeant was propelled upward. As soon as he'd gone up as far as he was going to go, he came down again.

It's hard to say how many branches the Sergeant hit on his way to the ground.

"Look out!" Mother shrieked.

Why she shouted this when he was already at the bottom of the tree I'll never know. Perhaps the words had gotten stuck in her throat and couldn't get out at the right time. Anyway, when she shouted her warning, the Sergeant was on the ground beside her. And so were Pat and I. We had come down the tree almost as fast as him. Of course, we didn't bounce around like he did. We came straight down.

"Oh, my Lord! Darling, are you hurt?" Mother asked.

The Sergeant was lying on his back with his eyes closed.

"He's dead," Pat declared.

But he wasn't dead. One eye came open, and he looked us over as though he were trying to place us.

"Darling! Are you all right?"

He sat up slowly and put his hand behind himself and applied a little pressure up and down his spine.

"I didn't break my back," he said. "That's the main thing."

Actually the Sergeant was hardly hurt at all, though he did walk like a wounded duck for a week or so.

Mother did her best to cheer him up and make him feel better. She smiled at him every time he hobbled past her, and at night she sang softly to him while she rubbed his sore spots.

That night I had to admit that living in the country was not always equally boring. I mean some days were less boring than other days. I liked the creek, and I liked Bounce. Yes, as an honest person, I had to admit that it wasn't completely bad. But I was still determined to escape from it. As soon as my escape fund reached the ten-dollar level, I would go. At that moment, it stood at only nine cents, but I took a vow that, from then on, half of all the money I got from my share of the bottles would go into the fund. I mean half of whatever I had left over, after the movie and just one bag of popcorn. And one bottle of pop.

CHAPTER SIX
Miss Scott

On the last day of August, the sky was overrun with low, gray scudding clouds. All the same, I counted it as a nice day. Lately I had begun to think every day that was not the first day of school was a nice day, because in a little while I was destined to go to a new school full of strange kids—the school in Station Hill. I was anxiety with shoes on.

After feeding the pigs and bringing the eggs in, I went for a walk along the creek. I was looking for a place deep enough to drown myself in, should things go as expected at my new school. When, finally, I wandered back to the house, I discovered that my aunt Margaret and uncle Max were there with a truckload of vegetables to get us through the winter. As usual, they'd brought Annie with them.

My cousin Annie was a year older than me. She was a very pretty girl, but looks can be deceiving. The fact is, she was only just barely a girl. She could swing from tree branches like a small ape, and she had a terrible temper. At home she had a huge pig named Oscar that she rode like a demon whenever she felt like it. She never played with dolls. She had no interest in them whatever.

After supper was over, Pat and Bounce went off to visit Violet Schneider, while Annie and I headed across the field to see if we could spot the badger who lived on the other side of the creek, down in the southeast quarter. The day was cool. Low gray clouds still blanketed the sky.

"Do you really think they'll like me?" I asked her. During the last five minutes, I'd asked Annie this question several times, but I'd not yet received what I considered to be a satisfactory answer.

"They'll like you!" she said with a flash of impatience. "They'll love you! Now stop talking about it, or I'll push you into the creek!"

As we slipped through the barbed-wire fence, I wondered absently if there would be other bad-tempered kids like Annie at my new school. Maybe there would be. Maybe I'd run into a whole bunch of them and they wouldn't like me.

"If they like me," I said on a positive note, "then it'll be okay."

In response to my moment of optimism and hope,

Annie turned around and said something that caused the blood in my veins to turn into chilled cranberry sauce.

"You'll find out on Monday," she said with a hideous smile.

At 7:15 on Monday morning, an old blue bus driven by the sad-looking Mr. Schneider and full of giggling, happy girls picked up Pat and me at the end of our lane. All of the girls belonged to Mr. Schneider. There was Violet, who was Pat's age, Rachel, who was mine, Wanda, who was in grade six, and Gretchen, who was in grade eight. There was also the golden-haired Catherine, but I had only seen her at a distance. She was not on the bus, because she was sixteen and went to the high school in Wistola with two other girls.

After several more pick-ups along the way, including my cousin Annie, the bus stopped on the road outside Station Hill School.

The school was a white building located at the southwest end of Main Street, across from the church. It had lots of windows, but it was not very big. It was near the front and center of a large open space bordered by caragana bushes on the sides, with a crooked pipe-rail fence in front. Behind the school yard, on the other side of another pipe-rail fence, there was an open pasture with a backstop made of rough timbers and chicken wire, in front of which a baseball diamond had been scratched out by usage alone.

There was no one playing baseball. My new school-mates were all milling about on the scruffy lawns surrounding the school. The boys were on the boys' side of the school and the girls on the girls' side. I entered the yard on the boys' side and stood there. My backside was against the crooked pipe-rail fence, which seemed to be vibrating at about the same rate as my quaking heart. A group of rough-looking older boys saw me and immediately huddled together in an intense, muttering group.

They're talking about me, I thought.

My little brother ran past me into the yard and instantly joined forces with a small group of kids of his own age. How I wished I had his knack for making friends. But I didn't.

The boys in the huddle went on muttering to one another and glancing ominously in my direction until, finally, there was a brief spasm of laughter. Then a big-chested boy with scruffy black hair left the others and came over to me. I expected the worst. However, much to my surprise, he grinned at me and asked if I wanted to play "kick the can" with them.

They weren't going to beat me up. This was going to be easier than I thought it would be. But as soon as the game of "kick the can" began, I made a startling discovery. I was the can.

"Ow! Ouch!" I screamed.

"Stop that! Stop that right now!" someone yelled.

As I grasped at my wounded shins, I saw, through eyes glazed over with pain, a young woman with short blond hair. My attackers scattered before her, for she was brandishing a willow switch, and in her flashing blue eyes was all the incandescent fury of the archangel Michael when, sword in hand, he fell upon the hapless Lucifer and his gang and sent them all flopping down to the lower depths.

"The next time anything like this happens," cried the fierce female, "it'll be the paddle for the lot of you!"

This threat had a powerful effect on my former assailants. They slunk further away, utterly defeated.

"Are you hurt?" she asked me.

I shook my head at her.

"I'm Miss Scott," she said. "I'm the teacher. What's your name?"

As soon as I'd told her what it was, she nodded at me.

"Welcome to our school, Donald," she said, smiling down at me. "This won't happen again. If you have any problem—any problem at all—you tell me about it. I'm in charge of this place, and I won't tolerate bullies. If I have to, I'll personally throw them out of the school."

After she'd gone, I limped back to the pipe-rail fence, accompanied every step of the way by a subterranean chorus whispering "Teacher's pet . . . teacher's pet." I didn't like what they were calling me, but I decided that being a teacher's pet was better than being kicked to death by a tribe of booted apes.

Presently Miss Scott reappeared on the front steps and rang the bell. A few seconds later, I saw that everyone was gathering in the vicinity of the empty flagpole, over on the girls' side of the school. I went there too and stood next to Rachel Schneider.

"What's happening?" I asked her.

"It's the official opening," she said. "Mr. Kruger does it. He always comes on the first day of school."

"Who's he?"

"He's the scoutmaster in Station Hill," she said. "Look! Here he comes!"

Scoutmaster Kruger was riding slowly toward us, sitting atop a beautiful chestnut mare and dressed in the finest scoutmaster uniform ever seen. It began with a well-pressed brown shirt and a scout neckerchief with a carved walnut slide. The big embroidered sash across his broad chest was loaded with merit badges from his own days as an Eagle Scout. His handsome brown riding breeches were so thoroughly pressed that they looked like they might be able to stand up and walk around on their own. A pair of shiny silver spurs were clamped around the heels of his gleaming high boots. A perfectly creased, wide-brimmed scoutmaster hat, with silvered badge, sat on top of his big head.

"He works for the government," Rachel commented, in an attempt to explain his splendor.

By the time Scoutmaster Kruger had tied his horse to the pipe-rail fence, Miss Scott had formed us up in neat rows, with the tallest at the rear, all facing the flagpole. Scoutmaster Kruger then marched directly to the front of the assemblage. He whispered something to Miss Scott that made her smile, then turned his beaming magnificence toward us.

"Good morning, boys and girls," he said.

"Good morning, Mr. Kruger," we responded in unison.

After the greeting, the highly polished scoutmaster

marched over to the white flagpole with military precision. He then fastened the Stars and Stripes to the line and raised it to the top of the pole. He stepped back, looked up at it, then slowly brought his gloved hand to the brim of his elegant hat. He then removed his Boy Scout hat and led us in a vigorous rendering of "The Star-Spangled Banner." Afterward, we all recited the Pledge of Allegiance together.

Scoutmaster Kruger concluded the opening ceremony with a message from the president in Washington, D.C. On behalf of our president, he urged us to respect the laws of the land, obey our parents and our teacher, be kind to animals, and not tip over Mr. Farquharson's outhouse this year on Halloween—especially if he was in it. On behalf of Benjamin Franklin, one of our great founding fathers, he reminded us that a penny saved was a penny earned, and therefore we shouldn't waste our pennies by putting them on the tracks for the trains to flatten.

Having gotten the school year off to a proper start, Scoutmaster Kruger then bid us adieu and rode off to run his part of the government. Later on someone told me that it had something to do with the government's lands and forests.

There was only one classroom in the school, just as Annie had claimed. One room with forty-three kids sand- wiched into it. It was fascinating. I'd never seen anything like it.

"Find your desks, then sit down and be quiet," Miss Scott said.

All the desks had a piece of folded cardboard on top

with a name on it. All you had to do was find your name, and that was your desk. Meanwhile, Miss Scott was busy settling my brother and the two other grade-one kids in their desks.

When we were all sitting in our proper places, Miss Scott stood in front of us. As she cast her eye around, a hush fell over the room.

"Sit up straight, Robert," she said.

After Robert was sitting up straight, Miss Scott welcomed the class and introduced the new students. These included me, a girl in pigtails, and the three grade ones. Miss Scott then raised the map of the world, which had been covering part of the blackboard, and a list of the rules of the school was revealed. She explained each rule in great detail so that there could not possibly be any misunderstandings. She next drew our attention to the bulletin board, which contained a duplicate list of rules for quick reference, in case there might be any doubt about anything. That settled, she moved back to the front and center of the class.

"For those of you who are new," she said, "we always begin our day with a song." She glanced at me and the girl with the pigtails, smiling as though she were about to let us in on a secret.

"Why do we like to begin our day with a song?" she asked, looking up at the class.

"Because music is the language of the soul!" everyone chanted. They knew the answer very well indeed, and they said it so loudly that I nearly fell out of my desk.

Miss Scott nodded in response. She then made a small upward gesture with her hands, and the class stood up. We all turned around while Miss Scott walked to the piano at the back of the room and sat down on the bench. There was a brief pause, then she began to play. A moment later, the whole class—except for me, the girl with the pigtails, and the three grade ones—burst into song.

The song was not like any song I'd ever heard before. It seemed to have something to do with "sailing the ocean blue" or something, but that's all I could get out of it.

The song was strange. The teacher was strange. The class was strange. The whole place was strange. I felt like I didn't know anything.

One thing I did understand. This was not the first time they had sung this song. They knew it by heart, and they fully enjoyed singing it. As for me, I wasn't enjoying it at all. While they were singing away with such gusto, I was wishing I were back in Wistola Elementary.

When the song was finished, Miss Scott stood beside the piano and smiled at us.

"Very good," she said. "You haven't lost anything over the holidays. Now, for those among us who are new, that lovely song was written by two very famous English gentlemen whose names are . . ." She paused here and raised her right hand.

"Gilbert and Sullivan!" chanted the class.

"Yes, William Gilbert and Arthur Sullivan, two of the greatest musical geniuses the world has ever known. And what kind of music did they write?"

Again she raised her hand, as though she were lifting up an old and well-known thought for the new kids to see.

"Operettas," the class chanted.

"And what do we do with their marvelous operettas?" she asked.

"We sing them!" the class chanted.

Pat and I were completely mystified. That is, at first we were, but we soon learned what it was all about.

It turned out that Miss Scott was extremely musical, and she strongly believed that music should have a major place in the education of children. As far as she was concerned, during the school hours we were her children, so, every day, first thing in the morning, schoolwork of the ordinary kind was left on the back burner, and she would sit down at the old piano. We then became the Station Hill School Choir, specializing in the works of Gilbert and Sullivan, those two wonderful English gentlemen that she so loved and admired.

"If everybody in the world sang in a choir, war would end and there'd be harmony everywhere on earth," she often said.

Rachel's sister Gretchen told me that Miss Scott had actually trained for a singing career and had only been held back from it at the last moment by her voice. I personally thought her singing was quite lovely, though it's true she would occasionally slip just slightly out of tune when attacking too long a string of dangerous high notes.

As for the rest of the school business, it was also very

confusing, at first. At least for me it was, because I wasn't used to it.

My biggest problem was that I listened to nearly everything Miss Scott said, and this was not a good idea in a classroom containing eight grades. The result was that I quickly became very confused about what grade I was in.

Although it was a close thing, I did eventually learn how to survive in that confusion. In time I learned how to know when she was talking to me—and the four other grade fives—and then to listen carefully. I also learned to close my ears and ignore everything else she said, except when she was speaking to the class as a whole.

We all had plenty of work to do, and most of us worked very hard. And most of us paid very close attention to Miss Scott's orders. And woe to those who didn't. For Miss Scott could move silently about the room, like an Apache in the night, and when she caught someone in the act of wasting valuable time—drawing airplanes in their arithmetic scribbler, or talking, or reading a *Little Orphan Annie* Big Little Book inside their history text—she would thump them on the head with her leather-bound copy of *The Poems of Elizabeth Barrett Browning*. It was not a pleasant thing to be thumped on the head by poetry, so most of the time everyone was very well behaved.

For more serious crimes, naturally the punishment was more severe. For the worst crime of all, violence toward another, the punishment was always the same, and the punishment was inescapable. It consisted of three or more good ones on the bum end, all solemnly applied in front of the class with Miss Scott's punishment paddle. The way it worked, you had to bend over and hang on to the edge of her desk with both hands, and then the paddle came down on your rear end. But that happened very seldom, and only for fighting and serious things like that.

After a couple of weeks of standing about at the edge of things, I managed to find a place in the outfield during the noontime baseball games. And slowly but surely I began to be accepted by the other boys, just as my parents had predicted. But had it not been for the peaceful regime maintained by the strong spirit of Miss Scott, they might have killed me before we had a chance to become friends.

Miss Scott was a dedicated teacher. Every hour of every day, week after week, month after month, all the year through until the summer holidays, she kept eight grades continuously busy, most of the time doing eight different things. As I watched her perform this miracle, she reminded me of the man at the Wistola carnival who kept eight plates spinning on top of eight thin sticks.

She also had the uncanny knack of appearing miraculously at the side of a student just when he or she most needed encouragement or help, and there was scarcely any kind of accomplishment by any of us that was too small to go unnoticed by her. However, it was impossible to fool her. She knew everybody in that room as if they were her own children, except for the few of us who were new. And, before long, we also became open books to her.

Miss Scott had the amusing habit of singing to herself

in a low voice. When we were all busy and things were quiet and she returned to her desk, we would, within a minute or two, begin to hear a muted version of "Poor Wandering One!" or some other little song.

It turned out that my brother and I both sang fairly well, and she taught us to sing a duet in French for a concert that was scheduled for next spring. Next spring was a long way off, but it takes a long time to learn to sing in French. The song involved a dog and a cat going to school in France and becoming famous for doing something to save Paris from someone called "Le Boche."

I soon came to like Miss Scott so much that I did everything in the world to please and impress her. As a result, my brain slowly began to get better.

"I like Miss Scott," Pat informed me out of a clear blue sky, one Saturday morning when we were out in the chicken coop gathering eggs.

For some reason, his innocent remark really annoyed me.

"I saw her first!" I cried, sending the chickens flying about in panic.

But Pat was no different from anybody else. There was no one around who didn't like Miss Scott. However, there was no one who liked her as well as I did—except, perhaps, for Scoutmaster Kruger.

Scoutmaster Kruger's government business required him to keep a watch over all the federal lands and forests in the area, and he spent most of his time cruising about the place in his gray government car doing just that. But the particular part of the land he kept the closest watch over was the small area containing Miss Scott.

Sometimes he drove up to the school during the last half of the lunch hour, and Miss Scott would go out and sit in the car with him for a few minutes. It was something I didn't like to see happening. Regrettably, as time went by, it began to happen more often.

One day after school, when we were sitting on the crooked part of the pipe fence, waiting for our bus to arrive, Scoutmaster Kruger pulled up in front of us and Miss Scott came out to meet him.

"Are they going to get married?" Rachel asked Annie as we watched Miss Scott get into the car and heard her laugh ring out.

"I hope so," Annie replied in a strange voice. "I think he's just dreamy." As she spoke, a perfectly dopey expression spread over her face.

"She won't!" I cried out so forcefully that Rachel fell off the fence.

While Pat and I were away at school during the day, getting to know our new teacher and our new classmates, life back at the farm went on without us.

Mother had her own problems to deal with, the biggest one being the laundry. When we'd lived in Wistola, she'd always used Mrs. Windemere's electric washing machine to wash our clothes. But since we had no electricity on our new farm, she'd suddenly found herself reduced to scrubbing clothes and things by hand, using a washboard and a laundry tub. Some things, like sheets and underpants, she boiled on the stove.

One Saturday morning while the rest of us were finishing breakfast, Mother suddenly smashed her scrubbing board. It happened right beside us, over by the stove. It wasn't that she broke it that amazed us, it was how she broke it. She broke it by raising it over her head and smashing it against the side of the washtub. After she'd done it, she ran into the living room.

"Your mother is tired," the Sergeant said to us after a long moment of astonished silence. "Stay here," he said. He then went after her.

Pat and I immediately went over to the place where the demolition had occurred and looked down at the remnants of the washing board. Pat picked up a piece of the corrugated glass and stared wide-eyed at it, while I surveyed the dent in the lip of the washtub where the scrubbing board had struck.

"What's happening?" he asked worriedly.

"I don't think she likes doing the laundry," I said. It was actually the first time in my life that I'd really thought about it—about what she did once a week, every week, all our lives. I suddenly felt very sorry for her. At the same time, I wondered what it would be like to never again have clean clothes.

A little while later, while Mother was sleeping, the Sergeant drove us to Mr. Kip's secondhand store in Wistola, where, after a lot of discussion, Mr. Kip showed him an ancient, gas-powered washing machine. The Sergeant tried it out before he bought it and it worked fine, even though it made as much noise as ten outboard motors. He then gave Mr. Kip five dollars for it, which was all the money he had. Actually he had twenty cents left, fifteen of which he spent on three ice-cream cones when we passed through Station Hill on the way back.

The washing machine consisted of a heavy metal barrel mounted on six sturdy steel legs, with an old gas motor at the bottom suspended between the legs. The metal feet at the bottom resembled an animal's hooves, but exactly what kind of animal it was no one could say. It also had an attachment that looked like a long tail, but this was actually a hose to send the motor's exhaust out the window.

When Mother saw it, she began to cry.

"See," I said to Pat. "They always cry when they're happy."

The Sergeant informed us that the washing machine was made in Germany. He proved it was by showing us an embossed bronze plate down near the bottom that contained the word *Deutschland*. This is the German word for *Germany*. What's more, the name *Siegfried* was painted on the side of the machine in strange-looking letters, and *Siegfried* was definitely a German name, the Sergeant said.

"They may have lost the war, but they know how to build machinery," he said. "This thing will last forever. It's built like a brick . . . outhouse."

Mother never referred to the washing machine by its proper name. She never called it Siegfried. She simply called it "the Monster" or, sometimes, "the Beast That Walks Like a Man."

The machine actually was capable of walking, and it would do so if for some reason it felt like it. At such times, it would usually walk into a wall and then keep on butting its barrel against it, until it was turned off and its load was adjusted. It was quite a frightening thing to see it walking around as if it had a mind of its own—a deranged one.

After trying it out in the kitchen a couple of times, the Sergeant went and got some lumber from one of the storage sheds. He then built a small laundry room onto the side of the house, so that the machine would have its own private place to walk around in.

But despite its frightening appearance and strange habits, and in spite of the terrible noises it made when in operation, the new machine worked well enough. It was certainly a vast improvement over scrubbing clothes by hand. Mother was content.

I wasn't content at all. I was still hoping that the bank would come and take the farm back so we could move back to Wistola, where washing machines ran on electricity and didn't try to go for walks by themselves.

In late September the Sergeant began to combine the crop of wheat that came with the place when he bought it. Each morning he had to get up early and go outside and beat the old combine into submission before it would agree to work. But eventually it would go. And, on the whole, it went pretty well once it was under way, provided its innards were regularly probed with a long steel bar, and provided its rear end was periodically kicked in the right place with a hard-toed boot.

When the Sergeant came back on that first night, after combining all day long, he was so completely covered with dust and grime that we hardly recognized him. He sat down heavily on a wood chair while Mother pulled a dipper of water from the pail and rushed it over to him.

"How's it going?" she asked.

"Good," the Sergeant said happily. "I've finished about twenty acres. I would have kept going, but it was getting damp and the combine was starting to plug up."

"I've made hamburger stew, and there's fresh pie for dessert," Mother informed him. "The kids have already eaten."

"Our teacher taught us a song," I proudly announced.

"That's nice," the Sergeant said absently. "I'll tell you," he went on, looking at Mother with a tired but meaningful smile, "it would sure go a lot faster if I had someone to drive Maggie for me."

"It's an operetta song," Pat declared.

"I'm not driving that truck," Mother said to him in a quiet voice. "If you need help, you can hire someone. I'm not a field hand."

"It's the Pirate King's song," I told them.

"You know as well as I do we haven't got the money to hire anybody," the Sergeant said with a frown. "Come on."

"Do you want to hear it?" I asked.

"Hear what?" the Sergeant responded.

"The song," I said.

"Anyway, I don't know how to use the auger, so I couldn't put the grain away by myself," Mother said.

"You could just dump it out on the ground, and I could look after augering it in later on," the Sergeant answered. "It's just that I don't have time to drive Maggie back and forth. It holds up the combining."

"Just shoveling it out of the truck," she said. "It would take me forever."

"No, it wouldn't. Ten minutes at most. There's a method to it. I'll show you," he promised.

"It's from *The Pirates of Penzance*," I declared.

"I'm not even sure if I could do it. I'm not a man," she said.

"It's not that hard," he assured her. "You just drop the tailgate and climb aboard and push the rest out. As much as you can. You can leave the little bits in the corners. You wouldn't have to shovel anything."

"It's one of the greatest operas in the whole world," Pat chimed in. "Our teacher told us!"

"Please," Mother said with a frown. "Don't ask me."

"It's not like you'd be the only one," the Sergeant muttered, looking down into his coffee cup. "A lotta women do it."

"Well, I'm not going to," Mother insisted as Pat and I went and made ready over by the stove.

"Well, then don't!" the Sergeant said angrily. "Let half the crop freeze because I can't get it in, and then see where we'll be."

At this point, having clasped our hands together neatly over our stomachs in the manner taught us by Miss Scott, Pat and I burst into song.

> *"Oh, better far to live and die*
> *Under the brave black flag I fly,*
> *Than play a sanctimonious part,*
> *With a pirate head and a pirate heart.*
> *Away to the cheating world go you,*
> *Where pirates all are well-to-do,*
> *But I'll be true to the song I sing,*
> *And live and die a Pirate King.*
> *For I am a Pirate King!"*

They both stared at Pat and me as the lusty song spewed forth from us. And it was clear from the startled expressions on their faces that they were more than a little surprised to discover that they possessed musical children. And although our voices may have wavered a little as we beat a path through some of the more difficult clusters of notes, we wended our way very determinedly through the whole song, from beginning to end.

When we were finished, they looked at each other for a second, then burst into a fit of laughter. I was totally flummoxed by their reaction.

"Didn't you like it?" I asked.

"Oh, no, we loved it!" Mother exclaimed, still sputtering with laughter.

After heartily applauding our performance, the Sergeant got up from his chair and headed for the washbasin, while Mother went over and stirred the stew. She gazed deep into the pot and smiled to herself.

"All right," she said. "I'll do it. But just this once. Just for this year."

He said nothing further, but when he'd finished washing he came over to the stove and held her tightly for a long time.

"What's your teacher's name again?" the Sergeant asked us after he'd finished his supper.

"Miss Scott," Pat and I answered in unison.

"Jean Scott," Mother amplified. "They say she runs the school with an iron fist."

"Good," the Sergeant commented. "There are too many flabby people in the world."

"They say she's sweet on the land agent," Mother added.

"No, she isn't!" I cried. "His head is too big!"

And they both laughed again.

That night I prayed fervently that matters concerning Miss Scott might be brought under control so that she would be protected.

"Please, Lord! Please make him go away!"

One day we came home to discover that the harvest on both our farms—ours and Cousin Annie's—was all finished. It was an immense relief to the Sergeant to have all his grain safely tucked away in the grain bins. And it was an immense relief to Mother not to have to drive and empty the truck anymore.

"I'll take it into the elevator later on," the Sergeant said. "Everyone's hauling now, so the price is too low."

"But what'll we do about the mortgage?" Mother asked worriedly.

"I talked to Laroque," the Sergeant said. "They'll wait a few months."

Mr. Laroque was the bank manager in Station Hill. His daughter Marjorie went to school with me. She was in grade six and she had very long hair. Once I asked Annie why her hair was so long, and Annie said it was because she was too stupid to cut it. I knew that wasn't true. Marjorie was not stupid. She was the smartest person in the school, and everyone knew it.

"What if the price goes down?" Mother persisted.

"It won't," he said.

"How do you know it won't?" she asked.

"It's the law of supply and demand," he responded.

"What's the law of supply and demand?" I asked.

"If there's a lot of something around, then the price for it goes down," he said.

"There are a lot of ducks around," Pat said. "I saw a million of them yesterday."

"He doesn't mean ducks," I said disgustedly.

"It might apply to ducks too," the Sergeant said. "If a person is in the duck business, then it would apply."

I wasn't interested in anything that involved ducks, so I went outside, where I sat down on the stoop beside Cannibal and rubbed his head for ten minutes.

We celebrated the end of the harvest with our relatives that night, but I was not in a celebrating mood. I thought that this success with the wheat might be enough to keep him going and we might never return to Wistola. I vowed to really start saving my extra bottle money, so that I could make my getaway as soon as possible.

At about this time the whole class began to make colored paper cutouts of outhouses and wheat sheaves and horses and tractors and other farm things, as well as witches, ghosts, and pumpkins.

"It's for the Harvest Dance," Rachel told me.

I thought nothing more about it until the morning, when Auntie Margaret came over to get some eggs.

"I'm looking forward to the Harvest Dance," Mother said to her.

"Are you going to it?" I asked, somewhat surprised.

"Of course," Mother answered. "We're all going. You and Pat too. Everybody's going."

"I'm not going," I said. In fact, I said it so instantaneously that she laughed at me.

"You're going," the Sergeant said from the other room.

The fateful night came, and we drove into Station Hill in old Maggie and then walked into the school. I hardly recognized the place. All the desks were stacked on top of one another at the back of the room, and there were benches along the cloakroom wall and along the window side of the room. The windows and all the walls were plastered with the outhouses and wheat sheaves and witches and other things we'd made during the last two weeks. At the very front, above the blackboard, big orange letters suspended from a sagging string said HARVEST DANCE 1946. Below that, the front blackboards were covered with the comic drawings that Miss Scott and the school art club had made on Friday afternoon.

A man with a guitar and a man with a fiddle and a pointed beard came and stood in front of the blackboard, to the right of the school piano. It had been moved to the front of the room for the occasion. A lady joined them at the piano, and they began to play country dancing music. I closed my eyes for a minute, and when I opened them, people were dancing all over the place, including my mother. Miss Scott, however, was nowhere to be seen, and I was glad, though I couldn't have said why.

"Do you want to dance?" someone asked me.

It was Rachel Schneider.

"Sorry," I said. "I don't know how."

I really didn't, and I resisted every kind of effort put forth by various people to persuade me to give it a try. Then Annie suddenly grabbed me by the wrist without asking permission and dragged me out to the floor.

"You dance like a jackass," she said contemptuously as she pushed me around the room. Although this was not the kind of comment likely to instill confidence, Annie insisted on teaching me all she knew, and as the night went on, my dancing improved. Indeed, it improved to the point where Annie hardly jeered at me. Presently I discovered that I was beginning to like it.

Later on, while I was dancing with Rachel, I encountered my mother being waltzed around by the Sergeant. They both smiled affectionately down at me.

"Nice to see you out on the dance floor," she said. "You dance very well."

"Ouch!" Rachel squealed a second later. "You stepped on my foot again!"

"Keep quiet or I'll take you back!" I hissed.

It was while I was spinning Rachel around the floor that I noticed Miss Scott standing by the door. She was wearing a beautiful blue dress, and her golden hair glittered in the lamplight.

"What are you doing? The dance isn't over yet," Rachel complained as I led her off the floor.

After I'd deposited Rachel on a nearby seat, I headed across the room toward Miss Scott. On the way over I debated whether to use "Would you like to dance, Miss Scott?" or "Would you care to dance, Miss Scott?" Really, there seemed little difference between them.

I never got the chance to ask Miss Scott anything. Before I was even halfway across the floor, out of the cloakroom came Scoutmaster Kruger with his big head, and without so much as a by-your-leave, he grabbed her around her tiny waist and swung her out onto the floor. And she laughed.

I took myself to a faraway bench, and there I sat in lonely anguish.

When I awoke in the morning, the sight outside my window made me forget all about Scoutmaster Kruger. The whole countryside was white with snow.

Miss Scott hated winter. Once it turned a little bit cold, twenty degrees below zero or thereabouts, she ventured outside only when it was essential that she do so. And before putting her nose out the door, she would hide herself inside a high-collared Persian lamb coat that was long enough and thick enough to see a sumo wrestler through an arctic blizzard. Underneath her coat she wore enough sweaters, scarves, skirts, and leggings to stock a Hudson's Bay Trading Post. A fur muff and a fur hat completed her ensemble. Once Miss Scott was fully wrapped up for an outdoor move, all that could be seen of her was a glassy stare between two scarves.

Unfortunately the Station Hill School was never warm at any time during the winter, not even when warming winds came over the mountains. The problem was that our school was heated by a coal space heater, which was left untended during the night. The result was that the fire would diminish and expire in the late evening, and by morning the air temperature inside the building was about the same as on the outside. At least it was for the first hour or so, but eventually the big Empirola heater would warm the place sufficiently so that we could take our coats off.

Depending on the kind of day it was and the temperature outside, there was even the occasional late afternoon when we would actually begin to feel reasonably cozy in our schoolroom. But not Miss Scott. Once the deep of winter had set in, she was never warm enough.

Sometimes, on a particularly frigid morning, Miss Scott would vow that someday she was going to move to Florida. We all knew that she was joking, of course, for Miss Scott loved Montana with all her heart. She would never leave it. She would never leave us.

One morning on the bus Annie came down the aisle and sat beside me. She enjoyed being the bearer of bad news, and I could tell from the expression on her face that she was bearing some.

"Guess what?" she said with a sly smile.

"What?" I asked.

"Miss Scott's going to get married."

"You're lying," I said.

"It's true. I went with Mom to the quilting bee last night, and everybody was talking about it. They're engaged. Her and Scoutmaster Kruger. Mrs. Peterson said he's even given her an engagement ring."

I found out what an engagement ring was, and then, with an aching heart, I confirmed to my own satisfaction that she did indeed have one. She wore it on her left hand, on the second finger from the end. It was a ring of gleaming gold, with a little diamond perched on it. The first time I saw it, my heart shifted in my chest.

Sometimes I actually saw the little diamond sparkle

when she held her hand up to the light from the windows. She held her hand up to the light from the windows quite often, as a matter of fact, and each time my poor, stricken heart shifted again.

After the diamond ring appeared on her finger, she sang with a heightened, joyful intensity, and it was quite apparent to me that all was lost. However, even though there seemed to be no hope, at night I still prayed that God might somehow save her from the scoutmaster with the big head.

With a sorrowful heart I heard that the wedding was already arranged. It was to take place in March, at the Station Hill Church, with the Reverend Hittle officiating.

"Guess what?" Annie asked me one cold morning in February.

"What?"

"Scoutmaster Kruger's been transferred to Alaska, so we're going to get a new teacher."

"You're lying!" I cried.

Losing Miss Scott to Scoutmaster Kruger was one thing. Losing her altogether was another. It couldn't be true.

But it was true. I made inquiries, and it was confirmed. Scoutmaster Kruger had indeed been transferred to Alaska.

So that was that. Miss Scott would marry Scoutmaster Kruger and she would move away and I would never see her again.

In my desperate search for some way to soften the terrible blow, it occurred to me that maybe now and then I could somehow manage to go over to Alaska and visit her, provided the place wasn't too far from Station Hill.

"After Miss Scott moves to Alaska, can we go over there and see her?" I asked Mother, after the Sergeant had gone out to check on the pigs.

Mother didn't answer me. She just burst into laughter.

"Why are you laughing?" I asked her.

"Don't you know where Alaska is?" she responded, still chuckling to herself.

"No, where?"

"It's two thousand miles north of us," she answered with a smile.

I'm never going to see her again, I thought.

"It's up there by the Arctic Circle," she said with a snicker.

Poor Miss Scott, I thought. She's going to freeze to death up there.

But Miss Scott didn't freeze to death up there. Instead she became disengaged from Scoutmaster Kruger, and he went to Alaska by himself.

Afterward, I wondered what all the fuss was about. I would soon be living in California anyway. It doesn't matter, I said to myself over and over again. It doesn't matter.

After Scoutmaster Kruger had departed for Alaska, a new Government Parks and Lands guy came to Station Hill. His name was Mr. Douglas Pierce and he drove about in the gray government car and he watched over the whole area. But the area he watched over most closely was the small area containing Miss Scott.

CHAPTER SEVEN
Farm Safety

The land was deep in snow, and I'd found a new way to pass the time. Mr. Schneider had cleared a large skating area on his slough, and I often went over there to skate. And so did some of the other kids who didn't live too far away. There were often boys playing hockey, and I played too.

There were problems, however. My skates pinched my feet, and I had no hockey stick. I asked for one, but the Sergeant said he couldn't afford it. However, he did build one for me by fastening a small flat stick to the bottom of a broom handle at the correct angle. It worked, but it didn't work very well. Even so, I was better off than those who used carved tree branches for sticks.

We'd been going to town with Mother regularly every Saturday, at which time she sold eggs in the market and Pat and I cashed in our beer bottles. These were the bottles we collected from our large stash at Charlie's place. So every Saturday, without fail, we went to the movies with Milton and my other friends. But I always made sure there was a little money left over. When I got home, I immediately went to the barn and climbed up to the loft and went to the far end of it, to the runaway can that I kept in the hay. There I would deposit what I had left. Sometimes it wasn't much, but it added up. In addition to the thirty-six cents I'd saved by myself, my uncle Max had secretly given me a dollar. So I now had a grand total of $1.36. I felt very happy whenever I looked into the can and counted it up. I was well on my way to the ten dollars I'd need to escape from the place. Yes, next summer I'd be living in Hollywood.

Of course, I could have used my savings to buy a hockey stick. I even thought about it once. But I didn't have enough. Plate's Hardware had the cheapest ones in town, and they were $2.49. Besides, I knew that if I broke my vow and dipped into my savings for a hockey stick, I'd do it again whenever I wanted something else. I'd be stuck out here forever.

One clear, cold night the Sergeant came in after several hours of working on the truck. His hands were frozen, or so it seemed, for he rushed over to the stove and rubbed them frantically to get the blood circulating again. I knew how he felt. I'd frozen one of my fingers the day before when I was playing hockey down at Schneider's slough. It hurts a lot when you thaw a finger out after it's been sufficiently frozen. However, the Sergeant didn't seem to mind his frozen hands. In fact, he was smiling.

"Elmer came by," he said, still smiling. "Prices are up a little. I'm selling it all."

"Thank God!" Mother exclaimed. "Now maybe they'll leave us in peace."

I'd lived in the country long enough to understand what he was saying. He was saying that the price of wheat had gone up and he was selling our crop. Visions of money in great quantities wafted through my head.

"Can I get a hockey stick?" I asked.

There was a long pause, during which Cannibal came out from under the stove, stretched, and went back under again.

"I don't know," he said finally. "We'll see what's left when we've looked after the mortgage."

The next morning the Sergeant cleared away the snow around the red grain bin and dumped a large quantity of wheat from the grain bin onto the ground. The auger was broken, so he had to shovel it by hand from the ground into the truck. I could tell it was hard work, just from the way he looked while he was doing it. Sometimes he would stop and press his hand against his backbone, as if he were trying to push it back into place. Later on, when he went into the house to get a cup of coffee, I tried to shovel some

113

of the wheat up onto the truck by myself. I managed to get a total of about three cupfuls of wheat up there before I gave up in disgust.

"Let me try," Pat said.

"You couldn't do it. It's too heavy," I said.

"I want to try," he insisted.

"Then be my guest," I said contemptuously. I then handed him the shovel, which was slightly bigger than he was.

He pushed a little wheat onto the edge of the shovel, then swung the thing around with such sudden force that the wheat might have actually made it onto the truck, if only he hadn't let go of the shovel. But he did let go of it, and it went sailing though the air like a silver spaceship until my forehead stopped it.

"You've killed me!" I cried. I slipped down into the pile of wheat, blinking wildly and clutching at my wounded forehead.

"I'm sorry! I'm sorry!" he shouted.

I felt quite numb all over, as if I weren't really there.

"I see three angels with golden trumpets," I informed him.

At this point he began to blubber.

"I think they're calling me," I said.

"Don't die," he cried.

"It's too late," I responded. "You've killed me, and now I'm going to die.

"They'll probably hang you," I added as an afterthought.

"Stay there! I'll get Mother!" he cried out frantically. He then ran off toward the house like his rear end was on fire.

My forehead did hurt a little, but I didn't really think my injury was very serious. I just wanted to make sure that Pat paid a reasonable price for his carelessness, that's all. But when I took my hand off my forehead, I was alarmed to discover that it was covered in blood. It then occurred to me that I was actually hurt. And hurt in the worst possible place too, for I knew that brain injuries are often fatal, and I knew that the forehead is right in front of the brain. If the wayward shovel had penetrated deeply enough into my head, then it was actually possible that I really might die, either from a brain injury or from the loss of blood. I grew more anxious still when I looked in the side mirror of the truck and found that my whole face was red with blood.

Just last week we'd had a government man visit the school to tell us that every year, without fail, oodles and oodles of very nice farm children are killed throughout the country by farm accidents. "Farms are dangerous places," he had said.

He was right. I stared at my bloody hand with horror and disbelief. Was I to be the latest victim of a farm mishap?

Meanwhile, Cannibal wandered over to my side to get his head rubbed.

"Go away," I said. "Can't you see I'm dying?"

By the time the whole bunch of them appeared on the

scene, I was sitting on the running board, staring morosely at my bloodied hand and wondering what heaven was really like. I sincerely hoped it would be like California. I had my heart set on going to California.

Mother took one look at me and went white.

"My God!" she said.

"I didn't mean to do it," Pat cried.

"Get him into the house," she ordered.

The Sergeant lifted me up as if I were a feather and carried me toward the house.

"I'm going to die," I murmured in a pale voice.

"Don't be silly," Mother responded.

"I've seen men live with half their brains blown away," the Sergeant said reflectively as we went up the steps.

"Well, this is not the time to talk about it," Mother declared in her acid voice.

"I didn't mean to do it," Pat cried out again.

"If we'd never moved here, it wouldn't have happened," I said quietly. I felt that death was very close, and I wanted my last words to strike home.

"Well, don't worry about it," the Sergeant said as he sat me down in a chair near the stove. "If you do die, we'll bury you in Wistola."

"Stop that! He's not going to die," Mother insisted.

As it turned out, I didn't die after all. In fact, once Mother had cleaned me up, it turned out that there was just one little cut up near the top of my forehead. I was amazed by the smallness of it in comparison to the gusher of blood it produced. We all were, I think. And that was when I first learned how much blood a little cut in the forehead can produce and how bad the whole thing can appear if the blood is spread around a bit by your hand. It could be a handy thing to know, in case invaders from outer space are killing everyone and you want to convince them you're already dead. Anyway, a tiny plaster from Mother's first-aid kit entirely covered my great head wound.

"You would have killed me if it had been a pitchfork," I said to Pat that night in bed.

But Pat said nothing. He was already asleep. He's probably dreaming about next year's ducks, I thought. I fell asleep very quickly myself. I was dead tired, having that day come very close to being killed by a farm accident.

The next day, after Maggie was full of wheat, Pat and I accompanied the Sergeant into Station Hill, and we drove right into one of the huge grain elevators. A red one. Our truck was quickly weighed with the load of wheat still on it, and then the grain was dumped through a metal grating on the floor. Maggie was then weighed again. The elevator man told me this was how they determined the weight of the grain.

"You do it by subtraction," he said. But I didn't quite get what he meant.

When I looked down into the grate, I saw that the wheat had already disappeared down a large, silvery-sided funnel hole, and it occurred to me that if the grate gave way I would definitely slide down into the hole and disappear into the darkness below like the wheat had done. The idea of it made me nervous. Having been badly injured the day before, thoughts of death were not far from my mind.

Though the town and everything was covered in snow, the Sergeant stopped at the store and bought us each an ice-cream cone in order to celebrate the first delivery of wheat from the farm.

"How come he didn't pay you anything?" I asked him later on, on the way home.

"They'll pay me by check," the Sergeant said.

"What's a check?" Pat asked him.

"It's a piece of paper you can exchange for money at the bank. But this particular check already belongs to the bank. It's been waiting for it like a wolf at the door," the Sergeant said glumly.

When we arrived home and piled out of the truck, we heard a horrendous banging noise coming from the house. However, by the time we had rushed up the steps and into the kitchen, the noise had stopped. A moment later, Mother emerged from the laundry room.

"Siegfried went berserk again," she said. "This time he nearly broke through the wall. He slopped half the water out."

The Sergeant began to laugh, so Pat and I followed suit.

"I don't know what you're laughing at," Mother said in a dry voice. "That thing could kill somebody."

This only made the Sergeant laugh louder. Then Mother began to laugh too, and we all laughed together.

"When the electricity comes, we'll get you an electric one," the Sergeant promised, after the laughter had finally subsided.

"What will happen to Siegfried?" Pat asked worriedly.

"Don't worry," the Sergeant replied. "We'll find a nice home for him."

Over the next two weeks, all the rest of the grain was hauled to town. It was sold at what the Sergeant said was a good price, but I didn't get the hockey stick I was hoping for. In fact, we had nothing at all to show for it, except that the mortgage was paid up and the bank let us stay on the farm. Actually Mother also bought a case of McIntosh apples and a bunch of other groceries, and the Sergeant bought a new tire for the combine, though in my mind it didn't deserve one.

And, oh yes, I forgot. The Sergeant bought a mean old bull named Roger.

CHAPTER EIGHT
The Refined Reverend Hittle

Once a week, on Sunday mornings, we all piled into Maggie and drove to the church in Station Hill. We'd done this nearly every Sunday since we'd moved to the farm. It wasn't that we were an especially religious family, but the Sergeant was convinced that the universe had to have a Supreme Commander. Mother agreed with him, and she also said it was a good way to meet people. As for me, I didn't want to meet anyone.

Uncle Max did not go to church at all. Uncle Max was a heretic. Although he played the bagpipes and was a high school graduate, he still refused to believe in God. He did talk about Him, though. In fact, whenever he felt like having an argument with the Sergeant after the Sunday dinner, Uncle Max would put his fork down on his pie plate and pat his lips with his napkin and smile across the table in a certain way, as he did one morning in November.

"Doggone it," he said. "How do you know there's a God? Have you ever seen Him?"

To which the Sergeant replied, "I fought all through France and Germany, and I served in the army for over four years, and you know, Max, I never once saw the Allied Supreme Commander. But I knew he was there."

I didn't understand Uncle Max's reply to this argument. I can't even remember what it was, but on the subject of God, his words never carried much weight anyway, since Uncle Max was doomed. Yes, everyone in the county knew exactly where Uncle Max was going to wind up. Because not only did he refuse to believe in God, he even refused to go to church.

Mother loved to go to the Reverend Hittle's little white church in Station Hill. She liked to get there early and find a good place up near the front, then she'd sit there smiling in her best dress and hat, looking very nice with some of her red hair showing. She especially liked it when it was time to sing the hymns, partly because she had a nice singing voice and partly because we sang standing up.

Mother was very fond of the Reverend Hittle. In fact, she thought he was wonderful. But not everyone felt the way she did about him. The Sergeant didn't. I once heard him tell Mr. Schneider that he'd rather spend three hours in the pig house than spend them in the company of the Reverend Hittle. There's even some reason to believe that the Sergeant only went to the Reverend Hittle's church to please Mother and, possibly, to do penance for the sins he might have committed if we'd lived in Wistola, where there were some.

The Reverend Hittle was a bony, waspish little man with thin, reddish hair and a small mustache. Speaking personally, I never thought he was enough to break an egg over, although Mother frequently told us that he was a very refined person. The Sergeant later informed me that this meant he'd been boiled down and sent twice through a screen.

Whatever else may or may not be true about the Reverend Hittle, he was a great preacher. When, in his Sunday sermon, he spoke about the goodness of God and the happiness of heaven, we could almost hear the wings of angels gently stirring the air in the rafters. Yes, he described heaven with such a lofty and inspired poetic vision that, given a choice, most of the congregation would gladly have abandoned their pigs and moved up there.

And sometimes it seemed we might almost reach the heavenly paradise on those Sunday mornings, when the light and joy of it was wholly revealed to us by the Reverend Hittle. Yes, at times it seemed that, with just a pinch more effort, the little white church might actually pull away from its foundation and ascend skyward. But then, just when our upward thrust had reached its peak, the Reverend Hittle would begin to speak of sin, of human weakness and folly, and the church would settle back down on its foundation. We were earthbound after all, held down by the heavy weight of our human failings. By our sins. And when he was through with us, we fervently longed to avoid those sins, particularly the ones we didn't understand.

Meanwhile, the dark and dreary Mr. Winter had crept fully into the land, and, having nothing to do, I was in deep despair. Then one day Rachel lent me a book called *The Wonderful Wizard of Oz*, which she had borrowed from the Wistola Carnegie Library. Then, later on, she lent me *The Cowardly Lion of Oz*, which she borrowed from the library especially for me, because I told her I liked *The Wonderful Wizard of Oz*.

I soon began to go to the library myself. I went on Saturdays, after the movies. There were many, many books in the Wistola library, but I wasn't interested in anything but the Oz books.

"You should try reading something else," the librarian said once, when I was on my way out with another armload of them.

"No, thank you," I said.

They had thirty-three of them in the Wistola Carnegie Library, all of them different. I read *The Emerald City of Oz* next, then I read *The Tin Woodman of Oz* and then *The Road to Oz*. For the rest of the winter, I would spend many wonderful hours reading all thirty-three of them at night, in the light of the coal-oil lamp, and they kept me happily occupied during the dark, silent hours of that first long winter at the farm.

My favorite was *The Purple Prince of Oz.* I wanted to be the Purple Prince and I wanted to live in Oz. As winter droned on, I began to dream that California would be like Oz and that Hollywood would be like the Emerald City.

It was late in November, after the Sunday service was concluded, that Mother got carried away and invited the Reverend Hittle to come out to our place for supper on the following Sunday. I remember the occasion well, because the Sergeant sat rigid and silent all the way over to Cousin Annie's; later, when we arrived home, he went out into the bitterly cold night and spent three hours cleaning out the pig house.

On the Sunday in question, Mother made a big roast beef supper with Yorkshire pudding, but by five o'clock the snow was blowing so bad outside that it was impossible to see two feet in front of you. Mother was in despair. The Sergeant, however, was quite cheerful.

"He'll come another time," he said with a smile, putting his arm around Mother to comfort her.

However, just as we were about to go ahead and eat without him, there was a weak tap at the door and the Reverend Hittle fell into our kitchen. Although he had a huge buffalo coat over him, poor Hittle was nearly done in.

"You shouldn't have come," Mother said happily. And while the Sergeant put on his boots and coat and mittens and went outside into the blizzard to put Hittle's horse in the barn, Mother sat the Reverend in front of the kitchen stove and poured into him all that remained of the precious brandy kept in the high cupboard in case of a major medical emergency.

It didn't take long for Hittle to thaw out. And, as soon as he was sufficiently restored, he accepted the place of honor at the table, whereupon he proceeded to eat enough roast beef to take a family of four through a depression. He mentioned early on that he had a particular fondness for the outside crusts of the roast—those very same parts that the Sergeant liked so well. On this occasion, however, the Sergeant didn't get any.

While Mother was serving the apple pie with whipped cream, Hittle began to talk about how old the Reverend Miller in Wistola was getting.

"I know him well," Mother said. "He must be eighty."

"Eighty-three," Hittle declared. "Eighty-three last September."

"He's very old," Mother nodded.

"He's in his dotage," Hittle replied. "He should have retired long ago."

"Do you think . . . Is there any possibility that when he does retire you might take over the Wistola church?" Mother asked.

At this suggestion, the Reverend's eyes fastened on our ceiling. When they came down, they were shining with anticipation and hope.

"Oh, I should think there is a tiny, wee possibility," he replied with a little hen chuckle. "After all, anything is possible, if our Lord wills it. And it is true that I have served this community with all my heart and soul for seventeen years and I am overdue to be moved. And it's also true that I have, on occasion, temporarily replaced the Reverend Miller in the Wistola church when he's had trouble with his liver. So perhaps there are some who do think that I will be chosen to replace him, in the event the Lord should call him from his travail. Or should he elect to retire voluntarily."

"I hope you do," the Sergeant said with no expression whatsoever on his face. "Kathleen, would you mind passing me a slice of pie?"

The Reverend Hittle's eyes narrowed a little, and he smiled at the Sergeant—rather in the manner of a stuffed vulture, I thought. Then he turned back to Mother and continued on with his prattle.

"However, I do pray that the Reverend Miller may serve the faithful flock in Wistola for many years to come, if the Lord wills it," he said in a syrupy voice.

"Amen," the Sergeant said, pressing his fingers into his forehead. "Kathleen, would you mind giving me my piece of pie?"

Later in the front room, as we sat in the circle of warmth provided by our Acme self-feeding coal stove, sipping lemon tea from Mother's best china cups, Hittle began to speak admiringly about the old Reverend Miller's big church in Wistola. He told us in detail how beautiful it was, how it was made of high-quality brick and had the finest organ and the most wonderful stained-glass windows.

"I know it well," Mother said. "We used to live in Wistola."

But Hittle didn't hear her. He seemed to be in some kind of dream state, and he went right on describing the Reverend Miller's magnificent church until we were familiar with every part of it. And as soon as he was finished describing the wonderful church, he immediately took us next door to its attached residence.

It was beautiful too, and made of the same red brick as the church, and the Reverend Hittle's eyes glazed over completely as he conducted us through the house from room to room, describing every marvelous feature of the grand place. And how inviting it sounded, too, with its lofty ceilings and its central heating.

When he mentioned the indoor sanitary facility, his eyes lit up with desire, and he lingered over its description, verbally caressing all the wonderful conveniences it contained—the sink, the bathtub, and, most especially, the lovely vitreous china flush toilet. He paused and closed his eyes, and a long moment of breathless silence followed. No one dared to interrupt it, for we all sensed the intensity of his feeling. It was as though Hittle's mind was struggling to go forward, was straining to take us elsewhere in the house, but was unable to move away from the marvelous bathroom.

Pat, who had fallen asleep against Mother, then made a small snorting noise, which startled the Reverend Hittle out of his fixation with plumbing devices. He came to himself with a sudden twitch and resumed the long and exhausting tour by conducting us mentally into the very ornate and spacious downstairs study.

"Such a study!" he declared excitedly. "It even has a leather-paneled prayer nook!"

At that precise moment it occurred to me that the Reverend Hittle fully expected to take over the Wistola church, that he was very anxious to move into its attached residence and to seize control of the sanitary conveniences and occupy the study. I sensed that he was no longer happy with the little white church in Station Hill, even though it too had an attached residence. True, the Station Hill residence only possessed two rooms, and it didn't have central heating or running water or a modern sanitary facility. However, on the positive side, it did have a fine coal-burning parlor stove and a very elegant two-hole outhouse, which was conveniently located under a nice Manitoba maple tree, at the far end of his backyard.

"Of course, I pray the Reverend Miller may serve his flock for many years to come," the Reverend Hittle concluded with a smile.

We soon discovered that the Reverend Hittle was also a poet. In fact, he had a small white notebook with him, which contained his most recent works, and Mother had no difficulty in persuading him to read one of his little poems. After a brief chuckle, he cleared his throat and began . . .

"There was upon a tree, a fig . . . ," which is the only part of it that I understood. Meanwhile, during the course of the fig poem, Pat again fell fast asleep against Mother. I was on her other side and I tried to fall asleep against her too, but she kept pushing me upright.

After two more long and incomprehensible poems, the Sergeant finally intervened.

"Kathleen, isn't it time for the kids to go to bed?" he asked.

"Aha, and I must be going soon," the Reverend Hittle said with a sigh, lowering his white book to his lap. "I only hope the wind has diminished. One can so easily get lost in blowing snow. I nearly lost my way coming here."

"Yes, it can be dangerous at this time of year," Mother said. "Especially at night. Perhaps—"

"I'll go out and take a look," the Sergeant interrupted, whereupon he sprang from his chair and rushed outside without even putting his coat on. When he came back, he was all smiles.

"It's almost calm," he said. "Lovely night! A little snow, but no wind at all. You could find your way home with your eyes closed."

I looked out the window and saw that millions of great white snowflakes were falling gently down from the heavens. But the Sergeant was right. The wind had died down. However, a few minutes after the Reverend Hittle left for home on his horse, the wind came up again. In fact, it began to blow with a vengeance, and soon all that could be seen through the windows was a mad whiteness of whirling snow. I wondered absently if we'd ever see the Reverend Hittle again. Then I saw something outside the window. It was the Reverend Hittle's horse, and he wasn't on it.

"It must've thrown him," the Sergeant said.

"You've got to go out there and find him. You can't let him die!" Mother exclaimed.

"No, I don't suppose I can, him being a great poet and all."

"This is not the time for jokes," Mother said dryly.

"No, of course not," he said. "Still . . ."

"I'll light the lantern for you," she interrupted.

The Sergeant quickly put on his coat and boots. He pulled his big mittens on, and, lantern in hand, he plunged through the door into the snowstorm.

We waited anxiously for him to come back, peering through the window every few seconds. And, a little while later, he did return—but without the Reverend Hittle.

"Don't worry. I'll find him. Just let me warm up for a second," he said, gasping for air and rubbing his half-frozen hands together. "It's worse than I thought."

"Why wouldn't he come back by himself?" she asked.

"He must have lost his sense of direction. You can't see two feet in front of you. It's that bad," he said.

"Couldn't you follow the footprints—or hoofprints?" she asked worriedly.

"There aren't any. The snow wipes them out as fast as you put them down."

"Oh Lord," she said.

"But I don't think he could have gotten very far," he said.

She picked up one of his hands and rubbed it vigorously.

"You be careful out there," she warned him.

"I'll be all right. I'll follow the ditch," he said.

"Take Bounce with you," she suggested.

On hearing his name, Bounce got up from his place beside the kitchen stove and came over to us. Cannibal followed along behind him.

"Yeah, I'll take him along," the Sergeant said. "Though I doubt he'll be much use. Now, if he were a German shepherd . . . ," he added with a faint smile.

A moment later, he stood up and wrapped his scarf around his face so that only his eyes showed. He then shoved his hat down over his head as far as it could go and put on his mittens. After he'd taken up the lantern, Mother held the door open for him and he went back out into the howling maelstrom. Bounce followed happily along behind him, leaping enthusiastically into the blizzard. It was as if he thought they were playing some new kind of game.

"Be careful!" Mother shouted after them.

After she closed the door, she made us kneel down in the middle of the kitchen, and we began to pray for his safe return.

"If he freezes to death, can we move back to Wistola?" I asked, between prayers.

"Never mind that!" Mother exclaimed crossly. "Just pray."

Sometime later on, there was a scratching at the door, and we heard a muffled bark.

"It's Bounce!" Pat shouted from the window.

It was Bounce, and he was alone. He was also completely covered with snow, and there wasn't an ounce of enthusiasm left in him.

"Oh Lord!" Mother exclaimed.

"Is Father going to die?" Pat asked as we watched her dry the dog off.

I had exactly the same question on my mind.

"No, of course not," she responded angrily.

And she was right, for, about half an hour later, a hoary, ice-encrusted Sergeant staggered into the kitchen with the Reverend Hittle. Hittle was wrapped up inside his Buffalo coat, and the Sergeant was carrying him over his shoulders.

"Here he is," the Sergeant gasped. "I found him in the ditch half a mile down the road."

"My Lord!" Mother exclaimed. "How far have you carried him?"

"All the way," the Sergeant gasped. "He said he couldn't walk."

The Sergeant set Hittle gently down on the warming chair next to the stove, then he collapsed on one of the table chairs, over by the window. After pushing his hat off his head and unwinding his scarf, he threw his arms across the table and laid his head down on them.

As things turned out, the Reverend Hittle didn't die. In fact, in less than an hour he had recovered sufficiently so that he was able to eat a few roast beef sandwiches and a small dill pickle. The Sergeant, however, didn't feel like eating anything. When he was able to rise from his chair, he just crawled up the stairs and went to bed.

The next morning, the sun was shining and the Reverend Hittle came into the kitchen fit as a fiddle and looking for his breakfast. But the Sergeant didn't come into the kitchen, and he didn't eat any breakfast, because the Sergeant was very ill.

"I'll send the doctor out as soon as I get to town," Hittle promised as he went forth into the sunlit day on his bony old horse.

"Pneumonia," Doctor Thorne said later on, after he'd finished examining the Sergeant.

"I'm so proud of you," Mother said a week later, after the Sergeant had recovered sufficiently to sit up in bed. "You saved his life. If you hadn't gone after him, he'd have frozen to death for sure."

"I hope he gets the Wistola church," the Sergeant said grimly.

I think it was mainly because the Reverend Hittle was poetic that Mother liked him so much. Mother was poetic too, being Irish. In any case, after the Sergeant had recovered from his pneumonia, she again invited Hittle out for a Sunday supper. After the supper came more poetry I didn't understand. Then she did it yet again on the Sunday after that, and before we knew what was happening, the Reverend Hittle had pretty much become a regular at our Sunday table.

Whenever Hittle visited us, Mother required Pat and me to be on our best behavior and otherwise do our utmost to prevent him from seeing what we were really like. This forced goodness was very stressful, so when Pat and I heard he was coming yet again, we went out behind the barn and began to swear at the snow-covered muck piles.

"Damn! Damn! Damn!" I cried out.

"Hell! Hell! Hell!" Pat shouted.

For we had both come to dislike the Reverend Hittle quite a lot. In particular, we hated the sound of his voice inside our house. On the appointed day, we stood out on the road and watched him approach, all the while wishing his horse would run away with him.

The routine of his visits was always the same. After the meal was finished, and Pat and I were thoroughly exhausted from dog paddling in a sticky slough of good manners, we moved into the living room. The Reverend Hittle thereupon reached inside his coat and took out his small white notebook. He then paid us back for his supper by reading his poetry out loud.

As soon as the poetry started, a fuzzy look came onto Mother's face and she commenced to smile continuously at the Reverend. When unobserved, Pat and I squirmed our faces and rotated our eyes at the ceiling. But the Sergeant neither smiled, nor squirmed, nor rotated. He sat rigid as a post on an uncomfortable wooden chair, with his hands linked on the rungs in back, and he stared at the middle of the Reverend Hittle's forehead until it was over.

Following the poetry reading, the Reverend Hittle usually took us on another exhausting tour of the Reverend Miller's beautiful church and residence in Wistola, stopping to examine the prayer nook and bathroom in great detail.

"It's a lavatory fit for a bishop!" he cried out on one occasion, causing Pat to sit upright and open his eyes.

Eventually the evening with Hittle came to an end, and when I went to bed I pushed one foot hard into the other. I held it there until the pain was great enough to blot the Reverend Hittle's voice out of my memory.

We knew he would come again, and so, in order to remove the Reverend Hittle from our life, Pat and I turned to the most powerful facilitator we knew of. Prayer. After every visit, that night, when we said our prayers, we'd add a short bit at the end in which we begged God to keep Hittle away from us. And one day, when we least expected it, our prayers were answered.

The wondrous event occurred on a fine, crisp day in December, when the Reverend Hittle arrived for yet another supper. On this occasion he beamed at us continually during the meal, and I sensed—we all sensed—that he had something on his mind. Later, after the pie was served, Hittle delicately patted his thin lips with his linen napkin and then emitted a long hen chuckle.

"I have some news," he said. "You'll learn about it soon enough, so I might as well tell you now. I've been given a new church."

"A new church!" Mother exclaimed. "The church in Wistola? Is the Reverend Miller retiring?"

"No, the Lord willed otherwise." Hittle smiled. "I'm taking over a church in Bemidji."

"Minnesota?" the Sergeant inquired brightly.

"It's not a grand church," the Reverend continued,

ignoring him. "It's not a brick church, and the residence is not elaborate, but . . ."

At this point Hittle broke into a huge grin.

"It has indoor plumbing!"

"When are you leaving?" the Sergeant asked him.

"I don't know," Hittle replied. "All I know for certain is that I'm going."

Later I carried the lantern while we escorted him out to his horse. We stayed there until he disappeared into the darkness.

"I'll miss him," Mother said tearfully. "He was so refined."

The Sergeant put his arm around her as we walked back to the house.

"He brought a little poetry into our lives," she sighed.

"Well," the Sergeant said as we reached the steps, "the Lord giveth, and the Lord taketh away."

After Mother disappeared inside, the Sergeant paused at the door and looked up at the starry sky.

"Taketh him soon," he said.

CHAPTER NINE
The Christmas Dollar

Christmas was just a week away. For Pat and me, it would be our first Christmas on the farm. For our turkey, it would be the last. I suppose the turkey's enthusiasm for Christmas was somewhat restrained, but for the rest of us, it was definitely the high point of the year.

It turned out that this Christmas was to be very special, because a little of Mother's egg money trickled down to Pat and me.

"I'm going to give you each a dollar," she informed us on Friday evening. "You can use it to buy each other a Christmas present when we go to town tomorrow."

That night, as I lay in bed next to Pat, a disorderly mob of Christmas presents wandered through my head.

"I'm going to buy you something really great!" I promised Pat.

"Me too," Pat said happily.

"Don't just say 'me too,'" I complained. "Say you're going to buy me something I'll really like."

"What?" Pat asked.

"I don't know," I said impatiently. "You're the one who's supposed to be buying it!"

"I know!" Pat said excitedly. "I'll buy you a bicycle!"

"You can't buy a bicycle with a dollar!" I objected. "Use your head!"

"All right, then!" Pat said in a loud voice. "What do you want?"

"I want you both to go to sleep!" said an even louder voice from the next room.

The next morning, while the Sergeant was down in the basement repairing our sagging foundation, Mother drove us to the city in Maggie, just as she said she would. She then gave us each the promised dollar and turned us loose on the glittering streets of Wistola.

"Now buy each other a nice present," she said in parting, "then come back here to the truck and wait for me. Don't be longer than one hour. Do you hear me? One hour."

Pat and I wandered down the street a ways and then held a brief purchasing conference.

"Make sure it's something I'll really love," I instructed

him earnestly. "And make sure you don't tell me what it is, or you'll spoil my Christmas."

We separated, and I began to make my way down Lincoln Street, looking in all the windows and wandering through some of the stores. I had no idea what to buy him, because I hadn't given much thought to that half of the project. What does a six-year-old kid like? I wondered.

As I slogged my way from counter to counter, I began to notice that one dollar did not exactly make me Mr. Howard Hughes. In fact, all the things I thought Pat would really like seemed to be out of reach. In Plate's Hardware, for example, there was a beautiful set of Chinese checkers with a red dragon painted on the metal board, but it was $1.49.

At last, after half an hour of wandering empty-headed through Flanagan's Department Store, I ran across a wonderful blue truck and made the discovery that it was only ninety-five cents. I looked at it for a long time and had almost decided to buy it, when I remembered that the Sergeant was planning to surprise us with two big wooden trucks that he'd been building secretly in his shop. So I wisely decided that the Flanagan truck might be one too many trucks under the tree. I put it back and continued to wander about and look at things until I was dizzy.

A few minutes later I was back on the street where I'd started, and I had accomplished exactly nothing. However, I had made one important discovery. I hated Christmas shopping.

As I stood on the corner and looked around in desperation, I saw Woolworth's beckoning me from across the street, and I headed toward it. Surely I would find something in there.

As soon as I entered the store, the odor of food hit me like a baseball bat. It was coming from my left, and I followed my nose until I came to their long lunch counter. On the other side of it, hamburger patties sizzled on a large black grill, while a huge basket of luscious, golden french fries sat dripping hot above a cauldron of boiling oil. Down a little way from me, a lady in a green apron pulled a large scoop of vanilla ice cream out of a freezer and dropped it into a tall, cone-shaped glass. Above me, in a long row, a whole series of brightly colored posters depicted all the wonderful foods that a person could buy, if only he had a little money.

As I fingered the dollar bill that lay sweating in the bottom of my pocket, I gazed with particular longing at a poster that contained a hamburger, golden fries, and a chocolate soda. All for the measly sum of thirty-five cents.

I knew what I was thinking was both wrong and dangerous. Besides, if I couldn't find a decent present for a dollar, what would I be able to find for just sixty-five cents? Still, there might be something nice for sixty-five cents. But then there arose in my mind the specter of a certain tall former army sergeant who, at that very moment, was at home in the basement, rebuilding the foundation of our house. And so, eventually, fear prevailed over hunger, and I reluctantly left the lunch counter and wandered deep into the store in search of the perfect one-dollar present.

I found it right away. At least, I thought I'd found it. A giant bag of marbles. Pat loved marbles, although he'd never actually had any of his own. But he'd seen them, and I knew he admired them. And these were perfectly round, glass marbles—a huge netted bag of them that would last him the rest of his life.

There was just one problem. The giant bag of marbles cost only fifty cents. It occurred to me that I could buy two of them, but who needs two giant bags of marbles? That would definitely be too many marbles for Pat to properly supervise. But if I bought only one bag of them, then what would I do with the extra fifty cents? That was the problem.

At last, after a great deal of thought, I came up with a way to get rid of the other fifty cents. I would buy something from the snack bar for thirty-five cents and put the remaining fifteen cents change in with the marbles. Pat would love that. Marbles and money mixed together. What a surprise! What a wonderful Christmas present! It would even look like a dollar's worth of present. And, most important, it was very unlikely that the Sergeant in the basement knew much about the price of marbles at Woolworth's.

I had the marbles in my hand and was looking for a Woolworth's person to come and take my money, when my eye spotted something interesting. It was a stand of ice hockey sticks at the end of another counter. Pinned in front of them was a large sign.

Now if there was one single thing in the world that Pat and I both loved, it was playing hockey with the other kids over on Schneider's slough. It was the one splendid, beautiful thing that made this long winter bearable, despite the cold and the snow and the frozen feet. Hockey! And from now on it would be hockey with a real hockey stick, instead of a modified broomstick.

My heart was pumping pure excitement through my veins as I threw the bag of marbles back and ran over and seized a hockey stick and bought it. I then began to fervently pray that Pat had not yet bought anything for me and that I could find him before the hockey sticks were sold out.

I ran desperately for the doors and was about to plunge onto the streets of Wistola shouting his name, when I saw him. He was sitting on a stool at the far end of the lunch counter. In front of him was an empty soda glass and an empty plate. I was just in time to see the rear end of a hamburger enter his mouth and disappear.

Pat was eating my Christmas present.

The sense of betrayal and outrage I felt at that moment almost lifted me into the air. It had never occurred to me that the little cheater would not spend all of his Christmas dollar on my present.

When he wheeled around and slipped down off the stool, he discovered my hot breath against his forehead.

"I got your Christmas present," he said. "See?"

He then held up a fat netted bag for me to look into. But I already knew what it was. Marbles! The rotten little swindler!

I vowed then and there that I would make him pay dearly for his treachery. Although I was too angry to speak at any length, I managed to get out a few key words: "I'm going to tell on you!" I cried out.

Pat's big brown eyes immediately filled with tears, but that did not work on me. All the way back to the truck, he begged me to keep the hockey stick for myself and not expose him, but my sense of justice was too strong for that. I would not listen to his pleas.

In my mind I saw a pleasing little scene in which the big Sergeant would look down at the cunning little thief and ask him to explain exactly what he'd bought with his dollar. And I would be there to advise the Sergeant about the cost of marbles at Woolworth's. This would teach Pat a lesson he should have learned long ago. Never, ever try to short-change an older brother. Especially when he's me.

"You were supposed to be back here an hour ago!" Mother said angrily when we arrived at the truck.

"Pat used his dollar to buy a hamburger and things!" I bleated.

"I don't care what he used it for!" she exclaimed. "I told you not to be longer than one hour! Now get in the truck! Both of you!"

Mother was so angry that I thought it best not to press my story on her. Anyway, I was satisfied to wait until we reached home. Then I'd seek justice from the Supreme Court. In the meantime, I sat back against the seat and watched Pat squirm in anticipation of his forthcoming hour of judgment.

As soon as we reached the farm, I leaped from the truck with all my anger intact. I immediately ran into the house and scampered down to the basement through the trap-door, expecting to find the great judge hard at work on our foundation. But he wasn't there. Then, suddenly, the light from above vanished, and I was alone in the darkness. Someone had closed the trapdoor on me. And locked it too, I soon discovered. However hard I tried, I couldn't force it open. I then sat down on the steps and screamed my head off, but there was no response. None. I continued to yell for help at frequent intervals, and after several long and dismal minutes had passed by, the trapdoor was finally unlocked and raised.

"What were you doing down there?" Mother asked me.

"Where's Pat?" I asked angrily.

"He's gone over to the Schneiders', I think. Why?"

"Where's Dad?"

"In the barn," she said. Then she looked down at me and smiled sadly. "Donald, I know what you're going to do, but I wouldn't do it if I were you. Your father . . ."

I didn't hear the rest of what she said, because I was already halfway to the barn by the time she'd said it. I was also seething with rage at all that had been done to me. I found the Sergeant by the stalls, getting ready to start the milking.

"You're just in time," he said. "You can milk the cow."

"But I . . . Pat . . ."

"Tell me later," he said.

Alas, before I could get my story properly organized, I found myself alone in the barn. Alone except for Goldie, who was waiting patiently for someone to unload her. I can truly say that, at that particular moment, there was nothing on earth to equal my fury. But a few minutes later, as I sat on the stool with my head against Goldie's underbelly and squirted milk into the pail, I found it hard to keep track of just how angry I was. It is a very soothing thing, milking a cow.

About half an hour later, I'd finished the milking. I then reached down under all that soothing and found the corner of my anger and pulled it back up to the surface. I stomped out of the barn, a pail of milk in either hand, once again breathing fire and utterly determined to bring Pat to justice. I went straight to the house, and after depositing the pails of milk in the pantry next to the separator, I marched back into the kitchen.

Pat was sitting at the table, quietly turning the pages of the Sears catalog and looking as if he didn't have a care in the world. When he looked up at me, I was amazed to see that there was not a trace of fear in his eyes. Nor did he beseech me for forgiveness as I'd expected. No, there was not a single pleading look.

Pat's complete lack of remorse was bad enough, but in the next instant he made everything a thousand times worse. He smiled at me. Smiled at me! After what he'd done, he actually had the nerve to smile at me? I simply couldn't believe it. It was the worst case of little-brother insubordination I had ever encountered.

My lower lip quivered in disbelief, and every fiber in my body felt the outrage of that incredible moment. Now there could be no mercy. Now I had no choice in the matter. I had a clear duty to myself and to all the other big brothers of every race and religion, in every quarter of the planet Earth. For them, for myself, for order and good government in the world-at-large, I knew that he had to be utterly squashed.

"Where's Dad?" I asked my mother, who was at the stove stirring a pot of stew.

"He's in the front room having a pipe," she said, glancing back at me. "You needn't bother to tell him . . ."

But I was far, far too angry to take advice from anyone. Even while she was speaking, I charged straight into the front room and told him everything. Yes, in one long, raging torrent, I told him the whole horrifying tale of Pat's greedy deception. When I'd finished the shameful story, I expected him to immediately call the little cheat in and punish him for spending my Christmas present at the Woolworth's food counter. However, instead of commanding my brother to appear before him, he simply smiled at me and waved his smoking pipe in the air.

"I know all about it," he said. "Pat told me himself when he came home."

I waited, not quite knowing what this meant. Had Pat been punished for his cheating while I was locked in the basement? What was going on? Then the Sergeant gave me a searching look and his smile evaporated.

"Tell me," he said, "when Pat offered to trade you the hockey stick for the marbles, why didn't you take him up on it? It would have been a fair solution, and then there wouldn't have been any problem."

I looked at him with a puzzled frown. Why was he going on like this? Pat was the cheater, not me.

"I'll tell you why," he continued, his eyes looking directly into my soul. "You refused his offer because you wanted to get him into trouble more than you wanted the hockey stick."

"No," I protested. "I just—"

"Yes, you did," he interrupted. "All you wanted was to get him in trouble. You could hardly wait to tell me what he'd done. Are you going to deny it?"

"Okay, I'll take the hockey stick," I said, wishing to bring this ominous discussion to a speedy conclusion. But he only shook his head at me.

"What Pat did was wrong," he went on. "Trying to cheat you was wrong, and he knows it. But what you did was even worse. He was willing to make amends to you, but you were so full of self-righteousness that you became a mean-spirited bully."

My head was swimming in a sea of confusion. I could not understand what he was saying. Was I not right in trying to bring the little criminal to justice? Is there no such thing as law and order?

"Then who gets the hockey stick?" I asked with a puzzled look.

"Nobody gets it," he said, "because nobody around here deserves it."

"But—"

"There'll be no hockey sticks and no marbles for either one of you. Not this Christmas," he said with a terrible firmness.

And so in that agonizing moment, I lost the one thing in the world I wanted more than anything else. The one thing that might make this country life bearable. But now it was gone. Now it was lost forever, because I knew that the Sergeant never went back on what he said.

I swore a blood oath then and there that as soon as the weather permitted it, I would run away to California. The realization of what I had lost brought hot tears to my eyes. What really galled me most was that it was through no fault of my own.

"No," I moaned.

"Yes," he said. "And I suggest you take a little time off from your temper and try to figure out what Christmas is all about."

I went away from him, knowing for certain there was no justice in the world.

And I decided that I would fight their unfairness. I would fight it until my dying breath, and they would soon regret what they had done! First I vowed to give Pat the silent treatment for the rest of his life—even longer, if possible. And then I went into a state of deep sulk, vowing to stay there until the weather had improved and I'd saved enough money to escape from this place forever.

It was not the best Christmas week I ever had. I was obliged to watch from a sullen distance as everyone around me enjoyed the happy season—the visits from friends and relatives, the goodness of Mother's kitchen with her busy in it, the anticipation, the spontaneous songs, and the happy chatter. Actually, I could stand all that, but the bone that really stuck in my throat was that none of them seemed to notice my silent rage. Pat didn't in the least mind me not talking to him, and Mother never seemed to notice how angry I was.

It was quite a difficult time for me. There was even one occasion when I was tempted to come back to life and join in the Christmas gaiety—the time when Annie brought her Monopoly game over. But I managed to keep firm to my purpose, and at least Annie noticed that something was wrong.

"Aren't you going to play Monopoly with us?" she asked with an astonished look as I put on my parka and wrapped my long scarf around my face.

"No," I replied as I pulled my mittens on. "I'm going outside to sit in the truck."

"I hope you freeze to death," Annie said.

Then came Christmas Eve.

After supper, the whole family, including our adjoining relatives, gathered around our Christmas tree in the living room to listen to stories and sing carols. I wanted to go outside and freeze to death in the truck, but I was forced to go into the living room along with the rest of them.

Mother stood under the glittering angel and read the story of Christmas in her beautiful, lilting voice, while Cannibal went from lap to lap in order to get his head rubbed by everyone there. Then Cousin Annie sang "Silent Night" in a voice that would have been quite lovely, if it had been in key. When she was finished torturing us, Uncle Max stood up and recited a poem by Robert Service called "The Cremation of Sam McGee" that had absolutely nothing to do with Christmas. And, following all this, they all began to sing carols together. Meanwhile, I strove mightily to fight off all the goodness, all the cheerfulness, and all the love that surrounded me. But it was too much to resist. Slowly but surely it closed in on me, and I felt myself enveloped by it, smothered by it, until, at last, the powerful Christmas light forced its way into my darkened heart and the darkness yielded to it. In the next instant I felt my mouth opening, and I began to sing.

Afterward, when the carol was over, I put my arm around my brother's surprised shoulders and gave him a sideways squeeze. Yes, my anger was all gone. The ordeal was over. But what's more important, I'd finally understood what it was I'd done wrong.

The Sergeant was right. I had been mean-spirited and petty. And not only had my meanness cost me the precious hockey stick, it had nearly ruined my Christmas.

I smiled at Pat as he looked up at me with his big, brown eyes.

"I forgive you," I said.

As I spoke, I saw that Mother and the Sergeant were watching me. They smiled, and I smiled back. All was well again.

"I know what we can do next year if she gives us another Christmas dollar," Pat whispered. "So there won't be any more trouble."

I could tell from the seriousness of his expression that he'd been giving the matter a great deal of thought, so I was very curious to know what kind of solution he'd come up with.

"What?" I asked him.

"When we get our dollars, we just trade them," Pat said with a gleam of triumph in his eye.

"Why? What good does that do?" I asked.

"Don't you see?" he said excitedly. "If we switch dollars, then you can buy your Christmas present from me and I can buy mine from you!"

I nodded. It made sense.

Later that evening, as we sat around the kitchen table eating some Christmas Eve dainties, Uncle Max smiled across the table at Pat and me.

"I heard you guys had a little trouble at Woolworth's last week," he said with a gleam in his eye.

Of course everybody in the whole country knew about the Christmas dollar fiasco, including Uncle Max. And since Uncle Max was the biggest tease in the whole world, I had been expecting him to needle us about it sooner or later. He would never let such an opportunity pass him by. I frowned in reply, and he grinned back at me.

"I gotta say, I felt sorry for you boys when I heard about it," he went on. He paused and looked directly at me with his eyes still gleaming. "Well, I'll tell you what," he said. "If you two go outside and check in the back of my truck, you'll find a little something that might cheer you up—a little Christmas present I think you'll like. Something I heard you had a hankering for."

How can I describe what I felt when I heard those words? Joy! Joy! JOY! For, of course, I knew what the presents were. Hockey sticks! A pair of beautiful, precious, brand-new hockey sticks! One for Pat and one for ME!

I glanced at my mother and the Sergeant, and it was confirmed. For I saw that they were smiling mischievously, and I knew instantly they were in on it with Uncle Max. It was one of those tortures old people like to inflict on the young. First they take away what you want, then they give it back to you in some tricky, roundabout fashion. They think it's funny.

A second later Pat and I were outside, running through the snow toward Uncle Max's truck. By the time I reached the truck and looked in the back of it, my heart was beating fast enough to melt the snow on my nose.

However, I didn't see what I'd expected to see. There were no hockey sticks. In fact, I saw nothing at all. Then I saw there was something. Sitting quietly in the middle of the truck box, half-covered in snow, were two identical netted bags that I instantly recognized. Marbles! Two bags of marbles from Woolworth's.

When we came back into the warm kitchen, the culprit

who'd deceived us broke into a huge spasm of laughter—
and so did everybody else, including Annie.

Some joke.

I did my best to minimize Uncle Max's enjoyment by
thanking him excessively and by pretending to be crazy
about the marbles. But it did little good. He saw right
through my act.

However, I was not going to let Uncle Max's rotten
trick destroy what little remained of my Christmas. No,
having once found the light after such great difficulty, I
could not let it go from my heart. And so, aside from wishing him a crop failure next year, I let the matter pass and
vowed to enjoy the rest of the evening, no matter how
much it hurt. So determined was I that I even played
marbles on the floor with Annie and Pat. And over and
over again, I told myself it didn't matter. But all the while,
disappointment gnawed away at my light, and toward the
end of the evening, I began to wonder if Christmas
shouldn't be abolished in order to safeguard children's
peace of mind.

At the end of the evening, just as I was about to turn
down the lamp and climb into bed, I heard a loud exclama-
tion of joy. It came from Pat.

I turned around to see what it was.

The clothes had been pushed aside in the middle of the
closet, and between them, resting against the back wall, all
festooned up with red ribbons, were two brand-new
hockey sticks. There was a note attached to one of the
sticks, which read:

God rest you merry, gentlemen.
—Mother and Dad

As we lay in bed with our beloved hockey sticks beside us, I tried to explain to Pat the significance of the note. This was not an easy thing to do, since I didn't understand it either.

"I still don't know what it means," Pat complained when I'd finished the explanation.

"Never mind," I muttered. "Just go to sleep. But remember, in the morning we gotta act real surprised when we see the trucks under the tree. We gotta pretend they're the best presents in the world. Even better than the hockey sticks."

"Okay," Pat said agreeably.

CHAPTER TEN
The Rites of Spring

It was after I became the owner of a real hockey stick that I really fell in love with the game. After the hockey stick appeared in my life, every spare moment I had was devoted to playing hockey down at Schneider's slough. During most of the winter, there was only a sliver of daylight between the time I arrived home from school and total darkness, but I used every second of it down at the slough. After school I usually played by myself, ragging the puck from end to end, with Rachel skating in large circles around me. I played ferociously every Saturday when others were there, and I played whenever I could on Sunday afternoons. Except when I was eating or doing chores,

I was down at the slough—if there was light enough and when the blizzard conditions weren't too bad. Sometimes I even played in the moonlight.

Often I would be the only one there, until Rachel spotted me from the white house and came running with her skates. Rachel and I had become good friends, in spite of the fact that she was a girl and didn't play hockey.

I had the time of my life for the rest of that winter, playing hockey without letup. I even played when chinooks came through and melted the ice a bit. Then one day, in the middle of March, a very strong chinook came roaring in, and the ice on the slough really began to melt. However, I wasn't going to let a little surface water stop me from playing hockey, so on Sunday afternoon I went down there as usual. I was all alone, but that didn't bother me either. I spent two happy hours sloshing back and forth across the melting ice.

As soon as I got home from school on Monday afternoon, I rushed out of the house with my skates and stick— as usual. The Sergeant was going in as I came out.

"I wouldn't skate on that slough anymore, if I were you," he said. "You'll go through the ice."

"It was okay yesterday," I informed him.

"Suit yourself," he said with a smile.

A half hour later I was back. I'd gone through the ice. I was soaked to the skin and nearly frozen to death. On the positive side—from my point of view—the slough wasn't deep enough to drown me.

"Lord Almighty!" Mother cried when she saw me dripping in the doorway.

"The ice broke," I explained.

The Sergeant was sitting at the table, and I fully expected him to say, "I told you so."

"You'd better get into some dry clothes and sit by the fire until you've warmed up," he said. "We don't want you to catch pneumonia." And that was all he said.

Sometimes he surprised me.

When I came back down, he stood up and took his coat off the hook to go outside. "We didn't mind the German bullets so much," he said. "It was the wet socks we hated."

Fortunately I didn't die of pneumonia, and on the following Sunday, I was still around to celebrate my eleventh birthday.

They had arranged a birthday party with a cake and hot dogs and pop, and I received presents from everyone. From my mother and the Sergeant, I received a brand-new pair of rubber boots with red rubber soles and toes. Pat received an identical pair, but his were smaller than mine.

It was Pat's party too. His birthday was actually a week after mine, but they decided to celebrate them together, in order to save money.

As for the other presents, Annie gave me a book called *Aesop's Fables*, which was the first book I'd ever owned, not counting our old Mother Goose book. From Auntie Margaret and Uncle Max, Pat and I jointly received a beautiful set of Chinese checkers. They were just like the ones I'd seen in Plate's Hardware during the Christmas-present hunt.

As soon as we were able to slip away from the festivities, Pat and I were outside, looking for puddles to tramp through with our new rubber boots. Having nothing better to do, Annie came along to watch.

There was no shortage of puddles. It was spring, and there was water everywhere. However, the biggest and best puddle around there was our little pond, and that's where we wound up.

We waded around the edge of it, back and forth, back and forth. Then we invented a new game, which would be called, "Let's see how close to the top of our boots we can let the water get without it going in."

It was a dangerous game, but a highly enjoyable one. Later, when we sat down on the steps to empty the water out of our boots, Annie gave us her verdict.

"You're a pair of idiots," she said.

We spent the rest of the afternoon inside, sitting on the living room floor near the Acme stove, learning how to play Chinese checkers according to Annie's rules.

That winter we seldom had any mail. Nevertheless, I had formed the habit of checking at the post office every day during the lunch hour, just in case someone might have sent us a letter.

Mrs. Zackary ran the post office, which was part of her general store. One day Annie came with me to check their mail, and afterward I asked her where Mr. Zackary was.

She then took me behind the church, into the Station Hill Cemetery, and she showed me his tombstone. Mr. Zackary was dead, it seemed. In any case, one day not long after my birthday celebration, I went over to the post office again, and, much to my surprise, Mrs. Zackary handed me a letter.

It wasn't just a letter. It was a letter addressed to me!

The letter was from my uncle Danny.

I'd heard all about Uncle Danny over the years, but I had never seen him in person. At least not that I could recall.

Before the war, he was a professional baseball player. He played first base, and Mother always said he might have made it into the big leagues if the war hadn't come along. But he quit the team and joined the Army Air Force the day after Pearl Harbor, and he became a B-17 pilot. On his nineteenth mission, he was shot down over Occupied France and listed as "Missing in Action."

There was a picture of him in the *Great Falls Tribune* at the time—a picture of him in his uniform, in better days. I remembered Mother staring at the newspaper picture and crying her eyes out. She thought he was dead. But he wasn't dead at all. He'd managed to bail out safely, and the French Resistance helped him to avoid capture by the Nazis.

Eventually the Resistance guided him over the mountains into Spain, and then some nice Spanish people helped him sneak back to England in their fishing boat. They hid him down below, where they kept the fish. It was said that Uncle Danny smelled like a mackerel for a long time afterward. He now lived in Boston, where he was a pharmacist with his own drug store.

I ran around to the back of the General Store, where I wouldn't be interrupted, and I tore the letter open. It was quite brief. It just said "Happy Birthday" and "Don't spend it all in one place."

The letter contained ten dollars.

I was rich!

I held the ten-dollar bill in my hand and stared at it. It was hard to believe it was really there. It was hard to believe it was really mine. In all my life, I'd never had so much money.

I was free! Now I could afford to run away to Hollywood and start my life over in a place where I wouldn't be surrounded by pigs and chickens, a place where there was no cow to milk, a place with indoor plumbing and radios and electric lights.

I could hardly wait to get on my way. However, I had been given a major singing part in Miss Scott's production of Gilbert and Sullivan's H.M.S. *Pinafore*, which was to be performed in June, at the end of the school year. In addition to that, she had taught my brother and me to sing a duet for the church recital in April. So I didn't want to let Miss Scott down by running away, because if I were caught and returned to her, she would strangle me.

It suddenly occurred to me that they used lots of kids in movies, and I thought there might be a movie that could use a singing kid like me. So the extra experience in Miss

Scott's productions could turn out to be very helpful to me, if someday I started a career as a singing movie star.

Aside from everything else, it was still very cold outside at night, and the roads were extremely muddy. It was not ideal weather for hitchhiking to California.

In the end, I decided to postpone my escape, until the odds for surviving the weather and Miss Scott were more favorable.

One day, late in March, the Sergeant used the tractor to plough up a large strip of ground near the house. The rest of us were watching him from the stoop.

"That's going to be our garden," Mother said. "We always had a great garden at home. Tomatoes and beans and carrots and corn and potatoes and everything else under the sun. You kids haven't eaten potatoes like the ones you dig up when they're small and new. They're wonderful! You wait. You'll see what I mean."

"When can we eat some?" Pat asked.

"In the summer," she said. "After the tops have flowered."

Pat was quite fascinated with the garden. He continued to sit out on the steps to watch the tractor go back and forth over the same ground. As for me, I went back inside with Mother. I was not interested in the garden. I'd already seen lots of them. There were gardens all over Wistola, and there was a big garden over at Annie's, behind their house.

Last summer Annie had thrown a tomato from their garden at me, because I wouldn't go with her to look at the beavers. Unfortunately I ducked, and the tomato went through the kitchen window. Uncle Max was not pleased, and he confined her to her room for the rest of the afternoon. A half hour later, when she was let out, she blamed me for breaking the window. She said that if I hadn't ducked, the tomato wouldn't have hit it.

Later that day—the day the Sergeant dug the garden with the tractor—Pat and I were up in a tree, and we watched him use Flight to spread a wagonload of manure over the plot.

"Look what he's doing!" Pat exclaimed. "I'm going to tell Mother."

I climbed down the tree and followed him to the house. I was just as curious about it as he was. Mother was in the kitchen, kneading dough for a batch of bread.

"He's putting cow crap in our garden!" Pat exclaimed. There was a horrified expression on his face.

"We don't call it crap," Mother calmly informed him. "We call it manure."

"Why is he doing it?" I asked her.

"It makes the plants grow better," she explained.

"Why?" I persisted.

"Because it provides stuff they like. When the manure breaks down, it goes into the soil and the plants can digest it."

"Eyaah," Pat said. "I'm not eating those potatoes."

"You don't eat any manure," she said reassuringly. "It all goes away. It breaks down into little chemical things.

The plants just take what they need to grow, and there's not a trace of it left."

A little later on in the spring, we all began to eat fresh radishes from the new garden, but Pat refused to eat them. I knew what he was thinking. But when the new lettuce appeared, he got over his problem with the manure and began to eat stuff from it. But he always regarded the garden and its processes with lingering suspicion.

Meanwhile, things had gotten worse at home because of the money shortage. At night, listening through the transom, I could hear their worried discussions. They had now fallen two payments behind with the mortgage, and the bank was very unhappy with them. So once again I began to think that we'd soon be moving back to Wistola and maybe I would not have to run away after all. But then the Sergeant sold his gold watch and bought a cheap brass one to replace it. He used the leftover money to keep going.

One day when I was sitting high up in the big tree, I saw him walking alone along the edge of the nearby field. I saw him take the brass watch out of his pocket and stare at it and then put it back. For a long time afterward, he just stood there looking out at the fields, like a post in a snowstorm.

If only we had stayed in Wistola. If only he would give up, then everyone would be happy. But he wouldn't give up. In spite of all the money problems, as soon as one of the fields was dry enough, he began to plant another crop of wheat and I began to think of running away again. But just at that moment, something happened in the barn that distracted everyone, including me.

We all knew that Goldie was going to have a calf, and one night in April, it began to happen. We were all out there in the barn to watch it come out, but I quickly retreated from the scene. It made me sick to my stomach. Afterward, Pat came running into the house.

"There's two of them!" he shouted.

And it was true. Our Goldie had given birth to twins. I saw them later in the day, and they were quite pretty, having been washed up.

"What are you going to do with them?" I asked the Sergeant as he cleaned the area up.

"I'll sell one of them and butcher the other. But not for a long time."

I left the barn more disgusted than ever with farm life. To me it seemed cruel and unjust that one of those two innocent little calfies would someday appear on our dinner plates. But I knew that I really couldn't blame the farm for that. I ate meat. We all ate meat. But it didn't make me feel any better about it.

Easter came, and we had our spring concert in the Station Hill church. It was nothing too special. Along with a couple of sprightly Gilbert and Sullivan pieces, there was a song in German, two songs in Latin, and, of course, Pat and I sang our French duet. Miss Scott had a love of foreign languages.

After the concert, everyone said that Pat and I stole

the show. I'm sure that's not true. Some of the others were fairly good.

It was during the spring concert that I decided I might as well wait until school was completely over in June before heading for California. This would mean hanging around for a few extra weeks after the operetta was finished, but there was no sense in throwing away a whole year of school and making Miss Scott mad at me forever. Aside from all that, summer is the best time to travel somewhere far away, especially if you're hitchhiking. In the meantime, my getaway money, the ten-dollar bill that Uncle Danny had given me, was safely hidden in a tin can at the far end of the loft. There were many times I was tempted to spend it, but I didn't.

CHAPTER ELEVEN
May Merriment

The day was warm and sunny, with a light breeze. The wheat was up and flourishing, and the tomato plants were about to go into the garden. Everywhere I looked, things were in bloom, or coming into bloom. It was Saturday, the twenty-fourth of May.

That afternoon Mother went to visit Auntie Margaret, and, having nothing else to do, I went with her. She drove into town first, in order to pick up a few things from Zackary's, and—wonder of wonders—Mrs. Zackary gave me a comic book.

The comic book was about someone called Andromeda Pilot, who flew around the universe fighting evil. That was all very well and good, but what really caught my eye was his beautiful rocket ship. Just looking at it made my heart beat faster.

The ship reminded me of a bomber airplane. I loved its long, streamlined shape. I loved the inside of it. I loved the cockpit at the front, with its pilot's seat and its control column. I loved its instrument panel, with all the dials. I loved everything about it.

All the way to Annie's, I stared and stared at the rocket ship. I stared at it so hard, I could almost see into outer space through its windows.

"Annie can't play with you today," Auntie Margaret said to me when we arrived. "Her father's confined her to her room for the afternoon. She's been a very bad girl."

"What did she do?" I asked.

"Never you mind," Mother said. "Just look after your own p's and q's."

"It's okay," Auntie Margaret said. "She threw her science textbook down the hole in the outhouse," she explained.

So Annie couldn't come out to play. Well, that was fine with me. I sat down on the steps and continued to devour the comic book, until Uncle Max came by.

"Mrs. Zackary gave me a comic book!" I said excitedly. "It's got a rocket ship in it!"

My excitement was transmitted to him, and he took the comic from my hands.

"Yeah, this is one great-looking rocket ship," he remarked after looking it over.

"I wish I had a rocket ship," I said with a sigh.

He looked at me thoughtfully and rubbed his chin.

"Why don't you build one?" he suggested. "There's lots of boards and stuff behind the garage, and there's tools and nails in the workshop. Just help yourself."

"Do you want to help me build it?" I asked him.

"Sorry. Can't. I'm on my way to town," he said.

Two seconds after he left, I was behind the garage with a hammer, a saw, a bucket of nails, and my Andromeda Pilot comic book.

I began the construction by dragging two old doors out of the scrap pile and placing them end to end on level ground. They would make a perfect floor for my rocket ship. I then carried two wooden boxes to the front of the ship. After nailing one of them to the floor, bottom up, I knocked the underside of it away. I then set the other box on top of it and joined the two of them. Afterward, I knocked out some of the boards from the front and sides of the top box. These open spaces on the upper box thus became the front windows of the rocket ship. I then placed another wood crate at the tail end of the ship, with the open end facing forward, and I nailed it to the floor. Next I dragged some old boards from the pile and nailed them across the open spaces between the front and rear boxes. I created a door into the ship by knocking some of the boards off the side of the rear box and tacking a gunnysack across the opening.

After the exterior was completed, I turned my attention to the inside. First I found a pilot's seat that had frittered away most of its life disguised as a butter box. I

168

carried it inside and set it in its proper place in the cockpit, a couple of feet back from the forward windows. After nailing a block of wood to the floor at the front of the ship, I fastened the top half of a broomstick to the side of it with a single nail, and it became my control column.

When I sat down in the pilot's seat to try the control column out, a strange and mysterious thing began to happen. As soon as I put my hand on the column, I heard a deep, rumbling noise, and the walls began to vibrate like crazy. My rocket ship was coming to life! It was as if I'd been transported to the Land of Oz and my ship had been infused with magic. I felt it shudder violently, then the low rumbling noise became a powerful, surging roar, and the ship began to move forward.

Yes, my rocket ship was moving across the pasture, gathering speed as it went forward, moving faster and faster, faster and faster. And then, wonder of wonders, the beautiful streamlined vessel lifted away from the dull earth and soared into the air.

Through the left side window, I saw the house and the barn and the garage and the trees and the outhouse. They became smaller and smaller as I was lifted higher and higher into the air. Now I could see Station Hill in the south and our farm in the north, both moving farther and farther away from me as I soared upward into the sky. Up, up, up I went in my beautiful rocket ship. Up through the puffy white clouds. Up into the high blue sky, where the thin cirrus dwells. Away from the earth I went. Into outer space I flew.

I flew past the half-lighted moon and soared outward into the solar system. As I approached Mars, I saw huge canals crisscrossing the red surface of the planet, and I saw the ruins of ancient cities. Past the red planet I flew, then I went by all the others, and suddenly I was sailing soundlessly through a great whirlpool of diamonds. I was in the middle of the Milky Way galaxy, with its billions and billions of stars. Away from the Milky Way I flew, into the unending expanse of the universe, with its billions and billions of galaxies, each with its billions and billions of stars, and those stars with their billions and billions of planets. Into the infinite, starry heaven I flew.

It seemed as if the universe would go on forever, but I saw, at last, the very end of it—the end of the universe. And closer and closer I came to it, until there was nothing but empty darkness ahead of me. And I thought that there was nothing else, nothing beyond the edge of the universe. But I was wrong, for I saw a vast form rise up from the darkness and come toward me. God?

It was not God. It was a horrible space creature. It was, in fact, the heinous Space Hydra, that vicious serpentine monster from beyond the galaxies. I thought she had been confined to her room for the afternoon, but it seems I was wrong.

I frantically turned my spacecraft around and fled in the opposite direction, but the Hydra came after me, striding across the galaxies until she was outside my window.

"Who said you could use Daddy's tools?" she asked,

poisonous pink foam issuing from the corners of her mouth as she spoke.

"How'd you get out of your room?" I countered.

"I opened the door and walked out," she replied. "What is this, anyway?"

"It's my rocket ship," I said.

"Rocket ship? This isn't a rocket ship! It's just a bunch of junk!" the Hydra responded with a ghastly laugh. And so saying, she pushed my rocket ship with one of her scaly legs, and the whole thing became bent in the wrong direction.

"Don't hurt my rocket ship!" I yelled.

Then she kicked it. The Horrible Space Hydra kicked my rocket ship.

"Don't hurt it!" I yelled again.

In response she gave it another tremendous kick, and my rocket ship collapsed on top of me.

"Eiyaghgghggh!" I screamed.

And then, like an enraged phoenix emerging from the ashes, I arose from the rubble.

"I'll get you!" I screamed.

"Yikes!" cried the Horrible Space Hydra, and she turned and ran away.

I ran after her, screaming at the top of my lungs.

"Help! Help!" she cried.

When she got to the outhouse, she threw herself inside and bolted the door.

I happened to have the hammer in my hand, so I ran

around the outside of the little building, bashing it with the hammer and screaming like a mad hyena. But already she was jeering at me from inside the smelly little fortress.

"Neyaw, neyaw, you can't get me, you stupid horse bun!"

The thing I loved most in the world had been destroyed by her, and there was nothing I could do about it. Nothing. Meanwhile, from inside the outhouse came another long string of jeers and insults. It was all very hard to bear. Then I happened to notice something. A long time ago my uncle had hammered a large spike into the edge of the plank door of the outhouse. This big spike was what they used to open the door, instead of a proper handle.

I hit the spike with the hammer as hard as I could and it moved inward, just a little. Suddenly I became a thing possessed! All my rage at the destruction of my beautiful ship, all my hatred of the Horrible Hydra, the destroyer of worlds, went into those hammer blows as I drove that spike inward. I pounded it and pounded it, and, finally, I drove that spike all the way through the heavy plank door and deep into the edge of the beam that the door closed against.

It was finished. I was done. I had imprisoned the Horrible Space Hydra for all eternity. In an outhouse.

I went back and surveyed the damage to my ship. It was very extensive, but I knew I could rebuild it. I resolved to make it even better than it was.

I went to work straightaway. I started by pulling it all apart, then I began the reconstruction. Meanwhile, the Horrible Hydra began to scream—very loudly.

"Let me out! I can't stand it in here! It stinks! Let me out!"

I ignored her and continued rebuilding the ship.

"I'll kill you when I get out!" she screamed hysterically.

I ignored that too, for I knew she would never get out.

A half hour passed quickly by—for me—and my reconstruction had progressed very well. My ship was nearly rebuilt. In the meantime, the screams and threats of the Hydra had degenerated into a sort of weak, mournful begging.

"I'm dying," the Hydra in the outhouse cried out in the distance.

Good, I thought. I'll bury you in a nice place by the hedge.

Within another half hour or so, my rocket ship had been completely restored to its former glory. Once again it was an airworthy space vehicle. Outwardly, at least. But it occurred to me that I needed one more thing to make it absolutely perfect. I needed an instrument panel like the one in Andromeda Pilot's ship, with all its interesting dials and instruments.

I ran to the garage and found a piece of cardboard, which I cut down to an appropriate size, then I headed for the house with the cardboard and the comic book.

"You're dead when I get out of here!" the Hydra in the outhouse screamed at me when I emerged from the garage. "Dead! Do you hear me? Dead!"

"Why don't you read your science book while you're in there?" I suggested as I went by with my cardboard. The

Hydra then became so hysterical that I could no longer understand what she was saying.

When I entered the hallway, I could see my aunt and mother in the kitchen at the end of the hall. Mother was holding a piece of chicken in the air with a pair of tongs.

I went upstairs and into Annie's room. I then used her precious crayons, together with the piece of cardboard, to create an instrument panel for my rocket ship. Slowly and carefully I drew each of the dials, then I drew the numbers and indicators. It was an enormous piece of work, and it seemed to take hours. But I really couldn't have been there much longer than half an hour, at most.

I went outside with my instrument panel and jumped off the stoop. I felt good. However, as I walked toward the garage, I noticed something was different. There was a deathly silence in the land. The Hydra was no longer screaming or moaning. A terrible thought then passed through my mind. Had she died from the fumes? Worse still, had she escaped? A cold chill went up my spine, and I suddenly began to worry about the future.

I walked slowly toward the outhouse, looking nervously all around me as I went. I approached the east side of it, where the knothole was. Then, when I bent down to look in the knothole, the cold chill made the return trip down my spine. The hideous green eye of the Hydra was looking out at me. And it was looking at me in exactly the same way that a vulture looks at a piece of carrion it intends to devour.

I hurried over to my rocket ship and was about to fasten my instrument panel in place when Uncle Max drove into the yard. When the truck stopped and the door opened, the outhouse began to screech in such a way that it raised the hair on the back of my head. I ran to the tallest tree and began to climb upward. Meanwhile, Uncle Max reached the outhouse and the screeching finally stopped. I heard the Space Hydra cry out to him in a sobbing voice. . . .

"He nailed the door shut," she said. "I've been in here for hours and hours. I'm dying, Daddy. I'm dying."

A very surprising thing then happened. Uncle Max began to laugh.

"I'll be right back," he said, still laughing. "Stay where you are."

He went into the house, and the others came back out with him. They laughed too when they saw it. At least, my mother did. For some reason, their laughter was a great relief to me. I even laughed a little myself, up there in the tree.

"Stop laughing!" Annie screamed. "It isn't funny!"

"Calm down. I'll get you out," Uncle Max promised. He went over to his toolshed and came back with a big crowbar, which he used to pry the spike out.

As soon as the door opened, Annie hurled herself out of the outhouse and fell to the ground, gasping for air.

"You poor little thing!" my aunt exclaimed, kneeling down and cradling her.

"The lentils!" Mother cried. "They'll be boiled to mush!"

The ladies ran back to the house, and Uncle Max sauntered along behind them, chuckling as he went. As soon as they disappeared through the door, Annie stood up and slowly looked around. Then she walked to the back of the garage, where she used the crowbar to smash my rocket ship to smithereens. Afterward, she picked my comic book up from the ground and tore it to shreds.

She gave the rubble one more angry kick, then turned and began to scan the trees with two beady, hate-filled green eyes. In order to resemble a large leaf, I tried to compress myself and make my natural skin color change to green, but she still saw me. She came to the bottom of my tree and looked up.

"I'm coming up there to get you," she said.

"I'm sorry," I replied.

She climbed the tree until she was nearly up to my branch. However, being unaccustomed to fresh air, having, until recently, been domiciled in an outhouse, she was suddenly overcome with dizziness. From the expression on her upturned face, I could tell that her brain was whirling around.

"Help me! I'm going to fall!" she screamed.

I didn't trust her, but I climbed down to the branch above her to get a closer look, and I saw that she was acting. However, it was very good. She did really appear to be in extreme distress. Her eyes were crossed, and she was wavering back and forth.

"I've got vertigo in my head and I can't get down!" she cried.

It was all very funny, and I moved a little closer for a better view of her performance. Regrettably, however, I went a little too close. Her hand came up like a striking cobra and closed around my ankle with a grip of steel.

"Gotcha!" she yelled triumphantly.

However, the sudden movement so unbalanced her that she lost her grip on the branch and fell from the tree. Unfortunately my ankle was still connected to her hand, so when she fell, I came down with her.

We hit the ground together with a dull thud. I lay beside her with my face buried in the grass. I didn't move. I didn't think I was too badly hurt, but I decided it would be best to pretend I was dead. She saw through it immediately.

"If you're dead, then I'm going to bury you," she said. "In the old well," she added.

"I'm not dead," I reluctantly admitted.

I began to crawl away, while she sat up against the tree to recover. Neither of us spoke for some time. I believe we were in shock. Finally I made it to a nearby tree and sat up against it. I looked over at her, and she looked back at me.

"I'm really, really tired," she said.

"I think I'm going to throw up," I said.

After a while, we felt much better. In fact, we felt quite cheerful and friendly, having just cheated death together.

"Someday I'm going to find the Lost Dutchman's mine," she said wistfully. "It's full of gold. Then I'm going to live in a big castle, with lots of servants. No trees."

"I'm going to go to Hollywood," I said. "I'm going to be a movie star."

"Let me know when you're ready to leave," she said absently as she stood up and brushed herself off. "I'll go with you."

CHAPTER TWELVE
The Picnic

On the second Saturday in June, the curtain went up on our end-of-the-year school concert. It was a lovely night. The sky was full of stars, and so was the school. The school was also packed with ordinary people—the relatives of the young stars—sitting on benches and chairs. The front of the room was a ship's deck, where the young stars proceeded to act out their parts and sing their hearts out.

H.M.S. Pinafore was a great success! The audience loved it! As for me, I wasn't the least bit nervous doing my solo, but I accidentally left a verse of my song out without even noticing it. It had just vanished from my mind.

Fortunately no one else noticed either—except for Miss Scott, who asked me afterward where I'd left my brain.

Two weeks later, it was the last day of school. It was June 28, 1947, a bright, blue-sky morning, with a light breeze coming from the mountains in the west. Everyone was anxious, happy, and excited, all at the same time.

Miss Scott rang the bell and ushered us inside, where we sat down at our desks and stared at the stack of brown envelopes on her desk. After a brief review of the year, we all went to the back of the room, one row at a time, to the school library. We went there in order to choose our "summer book"—as Miss Scott called it. The school library consisted of six shelves of books that had been donated by the community over the years.

I chose *Treasure Island* because the lady at the Wistola library had been describing it to me every time I took out another Oz book. She said it was full of pirates. Pat chose a book called *The Wind in the Willows* simply because he liked the picture on the cover.

After everyone had selected their summer book, we went outside and sat down on the grass behind the school, such as it was. Miss Scott then began to strum on her guitar, and we had a relaxed sing-along. Afterward we all drank a bottle of Orange Crush, which was generously provided by Miss Scott. We ate our lunches out there a little later on, while Miss Scott read us a wonderful short story about someone who was sealed up forever behind a brick wall. I wanted to change my summer book for the one she read the story from, but I sensed Miss Scott didn't like people who shilly-shallied about in making their decisions.

When the bell was sounded, we rushed around the side of the school and lined up in front of the flagpole. Miss Scott stood in front and smiled at us as though we all belonged to her. We sang "The Star-Spangled Banner," and, for the last time that school year, we recited the Pledge of Allegiance. Miss Scott then lowered the flag.

We headed back inside the school while she held the door open for us, smiling at each of us as we went by. Inside the classroom, she made a short speech about being honest, kind, and industrious during the summer holidays. She told us to have a nice summer and to be sure to read our summer book. Then her eyes shifted down to the stack of report cards, and a great hush of anticipation filled the room. She picked one of them up and looked at it.

"Do not open these report cards yourselves. Pass them directly to your parents," she said. She looked around the room and said it again, just to be sure we understood.

"Noah Bertleman," she said finally, raising her clear blue eyes to us.

Noah went up to the front and received his brown envelope. He grinned at us as he came back.

Pass? Fail? It could go either way for poor Noah. And for poor me too, I thought. I was very anxious. Annie had told me that Miss Scott passed or failed people strictly on their merits, without fear or favor. Annie had predicted my failure.

When my turn came, I was so anxious that my hand trembled as I reached for it.

"You worry too much," she whispered to me.

The process was repeated until everyone in the class had received their brown envelope. We were all chomping at the bit to see how we'd done and whether we'd made the grade or not, but we dared not disobey her repeated instruction. "Do not open it. Give it directly to your parents when you get home."

School was over! We filed out with our report cards, our summer book, and other things, and that was that. After a brief spasm of jubilation in front of the school, the town kids began to wander off. Ten minutes later, the bus arrived to take us home.

As soon as the bus got under way, we opened the brown envelopes and quickly drank up the information contained inside them. A great wave of relief went through me. I had passed into grade six! Not only that, my report card was the best I'd received all year long. I had made my way up the ladder, and I was now average in everything. That's what it said, and I was very happy with it.

The report was in Miss Scott's fine, clear handwriting, with letter grades of B-minus throughout. I believed every mark in it was accurate too, for Miss Scott knew every hair on my head and every thought in my brain.

"I passed!" Pat cried. "I'm in grade two!"

Annie passed, of course, as did Rachel. In fact, everyone on the bus had managed to move ahead to the next grade.

That night I heard Mother and the Sergeant talking about it through the transom.

"It's not that great," the Sergeant said. "Considering all the reading he does."

"It's okay," Mother said in my defense. "At least he didn't fail anything. And they both did better than last time."

"Yeah," the Sergeant agreed.

"Okay," Mother said. "So they're not geniuses. But they're doing their best."

"At least we won't have to worry about putting them through college," the Sergeant muttered. "They'll never get in."

And this started an argument between them that made it hard for me to get to sleep.

I was now free to head for California at any time I wanted. However, even with my chores, the days were pleasant enough. I saw no need to immediately rush away, just because school was over. Besides, in a couple of weeks there was to be a July Fourth community picnic in Station Hill, with free ice cream and pop and entertainments of every kind, including a baseball game. I did not want to miss it. Anyway, I needed to be fully rested before I started on my journey to California.

"Annie is doing acrobatics, and she's singing too," Mother said the next morning at breakfast. "It doubles her chances." She was talking about the talent contest at the July Fourth community picnic, where the best performance would win a money prize of five dollars.

Annie was always turning cartwheels and doing forward and backward flips around her place. She was a very good acrobat, like Mother said. However, I'd seen all of it I cared to see, especially since I'd once hurt myself badly in an attempt to show her that anybody could do it.

Anyway, she would never win the prize. No matter how good her acrobatic performance was, it would be canceled out by her singing.

"You should sing something," Mother said. "Maybe it's not too late to enter."

"No, I don't want to," I said.

I had no chance to win, anyway. Rachel had told me her sister Catherine was in it and that no one had beat Catherine in the last ten years. Anyway, I wanted to be free to fully enjoy myself, since it would be my last appearance in the community. I would be leaving for California very soon—no later than the end of August.

"Will there be ice cream?" Pat asked.

"Yes, there'll be lots of ice cream," Mother assured him.

"Right from the cow who makes it," the Sergeant chimed in.

"Do cows make ice cream?" Pat asked.

We all laughed at him and he laughed with us.

"Well, actually, you're partly right. Without cows we'd have no ice cream," the Sergeant said afterward. "You see, ice cream is made from cream, and the cows give us the cream."

It seemed to me that cows were involved in a lot of things, and I wondered where we'd be without them. There'd be no butter, no milk, no meat, no leather, and no ice cream.

Mother spent a good deal of time preparing her contribution to the July Fourth celebration. In fact, it looked to me like she was getting ready to personally feed the entire population of Station Hill and surrounding district. The food would be nice, but it was the ice cream that I really looked forward to. I loved ice cream, wherever it came from. Even when we lived in Wistola, I'd never been able to get enough of it. Out here there was none. Or next to none. Zackary's sold it, but I could count on one hand the number of ice-cream cones we'd bought there.

The day finally came. We put Mother's food into the back of Maggie, then we all piled into the front and headed for Station Hill.

"The Fryerton Eagles against the Station Hill Sodbusters," the Sergeant said, in response to my question about the forthcoming baseball game. "It should be a good game."

The celebration was on the grounds of the school, and the flag was flying at the top of the pole to mark the occasion.

As soon as we parked on the street across the way, I saw Annie running at us, with Auntie Margaret and Uncle Max waiting on the other side.

"You're already late," Annie said. "So you'd better hurry up or you'll miss the ice cream! Everybody's going around for the second time!"

That was all I needed to hear. I followed rapidly in her footsteps, while she pulled Pat along by the hand.

It was all happening at the back of the school, next to

our baseball field. A vast crowd of people were milling around out there. Old people, young people, babies—everyone in the town and country was there. There were tables crammed with every kind of food imaginable: pierogies and cabbage rolls, potato salads and Greek salads, buns and sandwiches, cakes and puddings, pickles and sausages.

A game of horseshoes was under way over by the hedges, on the boys' side, and the baseball teams were warming up on the baseball diamond, on the other side of the pipe-rail fence. Over on the right, on the north side of the school, beyond the food tables, there were three open tents. They were pitched in a row but well separated from each other. All of them had tables in front of their open doorways, with ladies hard at work behind the tables. Bottles of Orange Crush, Coca-Cola, and root beer were being handed out from one of them, with ice-cream cones from the other and hot dogs from the third. There were healthy line-ups in front of all three tables.

"Stop gawking and hurry up!" Annie shouted at me. She then broke into a dead run, with Pat flying along behind her like a small kite. I hurried along, but I did not run. I thought it was stupid to run after an ice-cream cone with hundreds of people watching.

The line moved very slowly, but eventually I walked off with a giant vanilla cone in hand. I soon had a bottle of pop in my other hand, and I stood there by the tents and licked furiously until the ice-cream cone was gone. I then headed for the hot dog table. As soon as the hot dog had disappeared down my gullet, I went back for a second ice-cream cone.

The baseball game was under way, and I wandered over to the pipe-rail fence and began to watch it, along with many others. It was interesting now and then, but it seemed to advance very slowly.

"I lost my finger," a small voice said behind me.

I looked around and saw that there was a little girl with large, dark eyes, about five or six years old. She held her hand up, and I saw that it had only three fingers. The longest one, or rather, the one that had been the longest one, was gone. Only a stump remained.

"I put it in Father's machine," she said, looking sadly down at it. "It chopped it off."

"That's too bad," I said.

"There was blood all over," she said. "My mother fainted."

I imagined her mother falling over, and I nodded at her.

"It didn't hurt at first," she said.

"Well, nice talking to you," I said. "I'm going to get an ice-cream cone now."

I went quickly, but she followed along at my heels.

"My mother's over by the tables," she said, pointing with a good finger. "Father wouldn't come. He said Station Hill stinks and they can shove it up their keister."

I hurried along a little faster, but she increased her pace to keep up with me. A moment later we stood together at the end of the ice-cream cone line.

I noticed there was a makeshift stage with a piano, over

at the far end of the girls' side. There were benches in front of it. That's for the talent contest, I thought. I turned my gaze back to the ball field. Over on the sidelines, some of the Station Hill Sodbusters had started to wrestle with each other while awaiting their turn at bat.

"I can still milk," the little girl said. "My finger didn't make any difference."

As soon as I received my ice cream, I walked quickly away from her and disappeared into the thickest part of the crowd. Then I doubled back and joined the pop line-up. I looked around, but I couldn't see her. I breathed a sigh of relief.

People were beginning to fill up the benches in front of the makeshift stage, so as soon as I got my pop, I wandered over there. I sat down in front of a line of big people, so that I couldn't be seen from behind.

There was a tent next to the stage, and Annie came out of it dressed in her red, white, and blue costume. I waved at her, but she didn't see me. She looked around, then disappeared back into the tent.

"Gears," someone said. It was the little girl. She was sitting beside me.

"What?"

"There was a hole in Daddy's machine and I wondered what was in there."

I didn't reply.

"There were gears in there," she said.

The baseball game was over, and the benches began to

fill up. Rachel and Pat appeared out of nowhere and sat down next to us.

"Hello, Joanne," Rachel said. "Don't tell me about your finger."

"What finger?" Pat asked.

Joanne held her hand up so that Pat could see the missing finger.

"I put it into Daddy's machine," she explained.

Without a word, Rachel and I moved to another bench, leaving Pat to his fate. He didn't seem to mind. He was fascinated by the little stump where the curious finger had once been.

When the benches were full, Mrs. Pilsner mounted the stage and sat at the piano. A fat, bald man in shirt sleeves came out to the center of the stage and looked at us.

"All rise," he said.

"That's Mr. Emsley," Rachel explained. "He owns the gas station. He's always the M.C."

"What M.C.?" I asked.

"Master of Ceremonies," Rachel explained.

With his hat held over his heart, Mr. Emsley led us in a stirring rendition of the national anthem, and he made a little speech about the meaning of Independence Day. After the speech was finished, he welcomed us to the annual talent show and made another short speech about freedom of the press. He then introduced Amanda Ivanovich, the first contestant. She recited a very sad poem in a very convincing fashion. The poem was about a little boy who'd died and how his toy soldier and his little dog were waiting for him to come back, only, being dead, he never would come back.

I liked the poem, and I liked the way she told it too. I especially liked the way she rolled her eyes around and looked up and down in order to express the feeling of what was going on in the poem. I also liked the way she pretended to wipe a tear from her eye during the sad parts.

As soon as Amanda was finished, Mr. Emsley announced the next contestant, and the flap of the tent opened. Lo and behold, out came Annie in her red, white, and blue costume. She walked calmly out to the extreme right side of the crowd, stood very erect, looked straight ahead, and then proceeded to do cartwheels right across the front of us. At the far side she stopped, stood straight again, then proceeded to do handsprings until she was in front of the stage, in the middle. Then, even as I watched, Annie turned sideways to us and began to bend backward until her head almost touched her keister. And she wasn't finished. No, for she now lay on her stomach, right down on the ground, and then she bent her head back and her legs forward until her ankles were on her shoulders, at which time she began to rock back and forth, like a living baby cradle. At the sight of this wonder, the crowd burst into spontaneous applause.

"She's double-jointed," I heard a man say.

After a series of backflips, she concluded the performance by walking on her hands all the way into the tent. My heart swelled up with the applause that accompanied her.

"You've seen the child!" the Master of Ceremonies loudly proclaimed up on the stage. "Now here's the father!"

And up onto the stage came my uncle Max. Yes, it was Uncle Max, and he had his bagpipes on. It then occurred to me that I came from a talented family. I almost wished I'd entered the contest myself.

Uncle Max began to play, and it was very entertaining—for people who enjoy the bagpipes. A little later he retreated to the back part of the stage and played the bagpipes for two girls in Scottish dresses who danced in front of him.

Another dance act followed, a little boy who performed something called a clog dance. He was replaced by a man in a brown suit, who sang a song called "Danny Boy." It was a sad song, and it reminded me of my uncle Danny. I wondered where he was and what he was up to, as I'd not heard anything from him since he'd sent me the ten dollars.

I thought about the ten dollars sitting in the can in the barn, waiting for me to take it to California. But there was no hurry. I had plenty of time. I could even wait until early September, if I wanted to.

Annie returned to the stage. For her second act she sang "Who Threw the Overalls in Mrs. Murphy's Chowder?" all the way through, from beginning to end, and she danced all around as she sang. I have to be honest. It wasn't bad at all. She might win, I thought. Then there'd be no living with her.

"Let's go get a pop," I said.

"Not yet," Rachel answered. "Catherine is up next."

Catherine was the oldest of the Schneider girls. I'd seen her around their farm now and then, but she went to the high school, so I didn't know her very well.

When she came out of the tent, she was wearing a white dress, and the sunlight seemed to spring forth from her long golden hair. For a split second just then, I thought it was Ozma of Oz mounting the steps up to the stage. If it wasn't Ozma, then surely it was some other fairy princess from that magic land. She moved lightly across the stage, then smiled at us and readied herself for her song.

When she began to sing, the hair stood up on the back of my neck and I stopped breathing. Her voice was as beautiful as she was. She sang a sad, lovely song in French called "La Vie en Rose." It made my heart quiver.

Afterward there was no doubt in my mind who would win the five dollars. And sure enough, a few minutes later the panel of judges, which included Miss Scott, declared that Catherine was the winner of the talent contest.

"She always wins," Rachel informed me. But I barely heard what she said, because my brain was completely riveted on Catherine. As she walked across the stage to receive her prize, a thousand stars glittered in her eyes. Her smile radiated out at me, and my heart beat faster.

We went off to get another pop, but the image of the golden-haired princess lingered in my brain.

After we got our pop, we wandered over to the area where Rachel said the "funny races for kids" were going to be held.

"There's prizes," she said, hopping along at my side.

"Prizes?"

"Ten cents for first place, five cents for second," she said.

At this point our conversation was interrupted by Annie, who grabbed me by the arm and dragged me away from Rachel.

"I need you for the three-legged race," she explained as she hurried me along to the racing area.

I discovered later on that the three-legged race was also called the sack race. In any case, my right leg wound up in a sack with Annie's left leg and then somebody blew a whistle.

It was a mistake to race in the same sack with Annie. I might have broken my leg. She had too much power. Anyway, she and I and the sack were soon racing far ahead of the motley crowd behind us, when I fell headlong onto the ground below. Although Annie dragged me the last few yards and threw me over the line, we still finished out of the money.

Surprisingly, Annie turned out to be a good loser, and she did not rip my leg the rest of the way out of its socket as I expected her to do. Instead, she wiped her eyes and told me we would win the wheelbarrow race. This was a distinct possibility, since we had been practicing it off and on all summer nearly every time I went to her place.

A few minutes later, we were all lined up for it. A man in a brown suit said "Get ready!" and everyone lifted their partners up by the legs.

"Go as fast as you can, but don't push me faster than I can go," Annie warned me.

At the same instant Annie spoke, the whistle blew. It caught me off guard, since my mind was occupied with Annie's comment. As a result, by the time Annie and I got underway, we were running dead last. For anyone else, our situation might have been hopeless, but no one could run on her hands like Annie. Before we'd reached the halfway mark, we'd overtaken everyone except for Casey and Cathy McGourlick. They were still several yards in front of us and going like a pair of banshees on a broomstick.

"Run faster," Annie screamed from below.

I ran faster than I'd ever run in my life while pushing a human being ahead of me, and we slowly closed the gap. And then, with the finish line just a few yards away, we were neck-in-neck with them. They tried their best to stay with us, but they faltered and we crossed the line first. The man in the brown suit congratulated us. He then put a shiny dime into my hand and into Annie's.

I was elated at my victory. I found Mother over by the tables, talking to some other ladies.

"Annie and I won the wheelbarrow race, and they gave me a dime." I brought it out and showed it to her.

As the afternoon advanced, the ice cream ran out, the pop ran out, and the hot dogs didn't taste the same. Over on the tables, the food supply had also been much reduced. I went over and ate a pickle. I was feeling a little ill, and I thought the pickle might help my stomach settle down while it digested all the stuff I'd eaten.

Someone made a speech over on the stage and suddenly the picnic was over. Before you could say "Jack Robinson," the tents were coming down, the food tables were empty, and no one was playing horseshoes anymore.

During the trip home I took my dime out to look at it, and it fell from my hand between me and Pat. I tried to turn around to find it, but we were sandwiched together too tightly.

"What's the matter?" Mother asked.

"I lost my dime. It's down there somewhere," I said.

"We'll look for it when we get home," she replied.

After we arrived home and everyone got out of the truck, I spotted the dime. It was stuck in the crack at the back of the seat. But when I tried to retrieve it, it slipped down into the crack and disappeared from view.

The Sergeant saw it happen, and he laughed.

"Don't look at me," he said. "I am not taking that seat out. The last time, I almost killed myself trying to get it back in again."

I looked so disappointed that it made him smile again. Then he reached into his pocket.

"Here," he said, putting a quarter into my hand.

I stared at the quarter. So far as I could remember, it was the first time he'd ever given me any money. Of course I knew that he didn't have any extra money—none to speak of, anyway. It had all been wasted on the farm.

A little while later, I hoisted myself into the hopper of the combine and crouched down at the bottom. I thought about the picnic and how much I enjoyed it. I thought about the beautiful Catherine. It seemed amazing to me that she was right now walking around inside that big white house down the road. I thought about how the Sergeant had given me a quarter to replace my lost dime. I thought about California again, and I wondered if Hollywood was really as great a place as it seemed to be.

CHAPTER THIRTEEN
Looking for Pat

One evening in mid-August, I was sitting on the floor near the transom and I heard them talking. They were talking about the mortgage again, and it was the same old story. They didn't have enough for this month's payment.

"Oh, darling!" she said.

"It's all that's left," the Sergeant said.

"Oh, no! There must be something else," she said.

"There's nothing left that's worth anything," he said in a glum voice.

"Well, if it has to be," she said, after a long pause.

"We'll get them back when the crop comes in," he

promised. "It's going to be a real beauty. There's no worry at all. We *will* get them back. I promise."

I didn't know exactly what they were talking about then, except they were going to have to sell something else and she didn't want to.

On Saturday he came to town with us. After giving Pat and me money for the movie, they went off down the street. Instead of heading for the movie theater immediately, I followed them until they disappeared into a pawnshop on South Railway Street. When they came out, she was crying and he held her in his arms. Afterward they walked together down the street, and at the end of the block, she suddenly laughed. I was glad that she laughed.

The movie was *Son of Frankenstein,* and there was a Gene Autry film along with it. I liked the Frankenstein movie. I liked all the Frankenstein movies. But as for Gene Autry, I never liked him very much. He had a bad habit of pulling out his guitar and singing, right in the middle of the movie.

Later on in the week, I found out that Mother and the Sergeant had sold their gold wedding rings. Annie had heard her parents talking about it, and she told me. I suddenly understood: That's what Mother had been crying about last Saturday.

I spent Friday morning lying in the hay at the back of the loft, with the great second-story doors open to the warming sun. I was reading *The Cowardly Lion of Oz* for the second time, and I was warm and comfortable and content. Cannibal came out of a pile of hay and lay down next to me to get his head rubbed. I rubbed it until I felt a hunger pain, then I gave it up and headed for the house.

Mother was in the kitchen, bustling about, getting lunch ready. In the little room next door, Siegfried was calmly doing the laundry. Over the last few months, she seemed to have learned how to tame him a bit.

The window was open, and a light breeze was making the curtains billow in. The Sergeant was already at the table.

It smelled like a bakery in there. Eight fat loaves of bread sat cooling on the cupboard. Alongside them, there were a dozen fat, crispy buns, and next to those was a great square of luscious cinnamon rolls.

"Where's Pat?" she asked me.

"I don't know," I replied.

"Well, lunch is ready. I think he's outside in the yard. Go give him a call."

I stood on the porch and screeched, "Pat! Pat! Lunchtime!"

"Is he coming?" she asked after I'd come back in and settled down at the table.

"I don't know," I said.

"Well, go and find him!" she snapped.

"And don't come back until you do!" the Sergeant added.

My feelings were hurt. I didn't like being yelled at when I hadn't done anything.

I went out front and walked part of the way down the road, toward Schneider's slough. I thought maybe he'd gone down there to check on the ducks, but he was nowhere in sight. I turned around just as Charlie came bumping down the road in his old Ford truck. He pulled up alongside me.

"Have you seen my brother?" I asked.

Unfortunately, I was close enough to get a whiff of the odor from the inside of the truck. I immediately took a step backward.

"Yeah, I saw him last week," Charlie said, and he burst into laughter. He thought he'd said something funny.

"I have to find him," I said with a frown.

"No, I ain't seen him," he said. "If I do, I'll tell him yer lookin' for him."

Without another word, he put the truck into gear and drove off toward town. I stood there alone on the road, halfway between the two farms, and tried to think of where he might be.

Ah, I know where he is! I thought.

While I was reading my summer book up in the loft, he'd been hollowing out a secret cave in the middle of one of the hay piles behind me.

I ran all the way back to the barn and climbed up to the loft. However, when I got up there, I found that he wasn't in his secret cave.

I walked to the end of the loft and again sat myself down between the great open doors. The whole of the countryside to the south was revealed to me. I saw Flight grazing out in the far pasture, but there was no sign of Pat anywhere. Of course I couldn't see through the trees, nor along the bottom of the creek. He could still be out there somewhere. I shouted his name several times, but there was no answer.

Cannibal appeared out of nowhere and climbed onto my lap. While I was rubbing his head and looking across the countryside, it suddenly occurred to me that the land I was gazing at belonged to us. It was our land. For some reason, I'd never thought of it in that way. Or at least, I'd never had the kind of feeling about it that I was having right then—that it actually belonged to me too. Or I to it. Or something . . .

I left the barn and wandered along the edge of the woods, screeching Pat's name every step of the way. I even went into the woods and looked up the big tree, but he wasn't up there either. I then hiked back to the middle of the yard and turned through every point in the compass, screaming his name as I rotated.

"Pat! Pat! Pat! Pat! Pat! Pat! Pat!"

Bounce came bounding out of the woods in response to my shouts. He ran across the yard toward me. Aha! So Pat was in the woods after all. Yes, I knew he had to be hiding somewhere in there, because Bounce was always with him when he was outside.

"Go find him, Bounce!" I commanded. Bounce seemed very willing to help. He went bounding back into the woods, pausing every now and then to make sure I was still with him. I followed him deep into the woods, and presently I walked out on the far side. I frowned at him.

"He isn't out here!" I said, looking at the fields.

There was a slight tone of rebuke in my voice, and Bounce, being extremely sensitive, thought he'd detected it. He drooped down to the ground and whimpered.

"It's okay, boy," I reassured him. I thought that perhaps he didn't understand what was wanted of him, so I repeated the command more precisely.

"Go find Pat! Find Pat!"

Bounce responded immediately, and there was something new in his manner that made me believe that he did know where Pat was. For he was not bouncing around like he usually did. No, he was going around in circles in a businesslike fashion, with his nose right to the ground and sniffing very purposefully. Finally he was on the trail of my missing brother. Only it seemed that the trail did not lead back into the woods. It went straight ahead, into the wheat field. I hesitated then, for I could see right across the field, and I could not see Pat. Then I heard my mother's voice in my brain.

Find him! it said.

I followed Bounce into the field, bellowing like a bull as I went.

"Pat! Pat! Pat! Pat! Pat! Pat! Pat! Pat!"

By the time I had walked across the whole field, I was growing quite impatient with Bounce.

"Where is he, then?" I shouted at him.

Bounce immediately fell to the ground and rolled over, sticking his feet in the air.

He always did this when he thought he was in trouble. The Sergeant said it was something called the "submissive posture." Among wolf packs, the lesser wolves submit to the leader by groveling in this manner. I looked at Bounce very closely, but I couldn't see any wolf in him—only cowardice.

"Get up!" I said in a tone of disgust.

He didn't get up. He merely rolled over and slithered up to my shoes like an apologetic snake.

"All right, come on," I said in a tone of renewed friendship. In response to this, he jumped happily upward and went bounding ahead of me. He ran under the barbed wire into the pasture, then turned around and grinned at me.

"Not that way," I yelled. "We're going back."

Then Bounce did a strange thing. He let out a muffled bark and made a little jump, then skittered off a little farther into the pasture. Then he turned around and made a bunch of little jumps in the air, as though he was urging me to follow him. But I stood my ground. He didn't fool me. He didn't know where Pat was any more than I did. Or did he?

Was it possible that Pat was somewhere along the creek?

"Pat!"

I scrambled through the fence and ran at top speed across the pasture. Bounce, when he saw me coming toward him like that, threw himself to the ground and began to grovel. I ran past him and kept running until I reached the far bush, by the creek. Even then I did not stop. I didn't stop until I arrived breathless at the bend in the creek.

"Pat!!" I roared. "Pat!!!"

But there was no response.

The big pond! He might be there. That's where we often went on hot days like this. Actually, he was not supposed to go to the big pond by himself, because he was too young to swim alone. He had the kind of freewheeling personality that often gets drowned.

I had a sudden vision of Pat lying in an open coffin, with his hands folded across his chest and a white flower laid over them. When I leaned over the coffin to look more closely, I saw there were pennies in his eyes. A cold shudder ran down my spine.

Suddenly I had a bad feeling about him. I had a feeling that I might find his corpse floating in the pond. I walked rapidly upstream until I was standing on the grassy bank, above the quiet water of the pond. No Pat. No beaver. No nothing. The pond was still and tranquil.

I frowned and sat down on the bank. "Where is he?" I asked quietly. In response to what he thought was a compliment, Bounce began to lick my face.

It was a hot day, and I'd made it hotter by rushing hither and thither and yon. I wiped the sweat from my forehead and looked down at the pond. A frog leaped off a rock and landed in the cool water.

A moment later, as I floated out toward the center of the pond, I could feel the water getting colder. I shuddered involuntarily. One of the drawbacks of our creek was that the water tended to be too cold, even on a hot day like this. It was almost ice water where it started up out of the ground five miles away, and since the banks were mostly lined with bushes and trees, their shade helped to keep it cold as it meandered along.

On the far shore of the pond, however, there was a mud shallow that was exposed to the afternoon sun, and there it could get very warm—almost hot. It was a pond full of extremes.

In a little while I remembered that I was supposed to be looking for Pat, so I climbed out of the water and slipped out of my shorts and into my trousers. I placed the shorts on a bush and lay down on the grassy bank to wait for them to dry.

"Pat!" I screamed. Still no answer.

I never swam naked, because I always had the feeling there could be girls lurking in the saskatoon bushes up on the hill, spying on me. I knew that girls did that sort of thing. Annie told me that she did it, and she was a girl. More or less.

"Pat!" I screeched.

When my shorts were dry and I was ready to go, I noticed that Bounce was looking hard upstream. It was like he was trying to point, almost. The Sergeant had once said that he had some pointer in him. But where was he pointing? Ah, he was pointing in the direction of the old hermit's shack. Could Pat be there?

I trudged farther up the creek while Bounce leaped ahead of me. I think he wanted to see the Hermit again.

As we approached the shack, the door opened and the old man waved us inside.

"I'm looking for my brother," I said.

"I haven't seen him," he said. "Sit down, lad. You look tuckered out. I'll make us some tea. Are you hungry?"

I'd not yet had my lunch, and all that hiking and yelling had caused my appetite to rise up in me, so I nodded my head as I sat down on the cot. The Hermit then reached into his food box and brought out a large jar, half full of dried fish.

"Here," he said, handing me the jar. "You can have some of my smoked trout."

When I looked down into the jar, I thought I saw a small cobweb in there with the fish. It was just my imagination working overtime, but I was still doubtful about eating any of the trout. With or without a cobweb, they looked as if they might be a bit past their prime. When I hesitated, the Hermit smiled understandingly and patted my head.

"No need to be polite around me." He laughed. "Go ahead. Eat as much as you like. I want to get rid of them before they spoil."

I tried a small piece and discovered that dried fish is much tastier than it looks. In fact, the Hermit's dried fish was delicious. Later, after I'd eaten about a pound and a half of his smoked fish and had just begun to gnaw at the rocklike edge of one of his biscuits, the Hermit lit up his pipe and pushed his chair back on its hind legs until it rested against the table.

"Yup! Yup! That reminds me of the time Larry and me was off from the war," he said.

"My grandfather was killed in that war," I informed him.

"Yup, yup, lots of 'em were. Anyway, me and Larry, we were taking a little holiday from it, like. That was . . . let's see . . . in seventeen or eighteen. In Morocco. At Rabat. We was in the quarter, and Larry says . . . he says, 'The Sheik of Rabat lives up there! I know him,' he says. 'We'll go up there,' he says. So we goes up, and the Sheik gives us coffee. That's their drink, all right! Coffee. You know how they love coffee?"

I looked at him and shook my head.

"Well, they love it! Drink it all the time. But you got to know how to do it or you'll hurt their feelings, and that isn't good. You got to sip it. Drink it all down in one gulp and it's an insult. Anyway, me and Larry's drinking coffee—sippin' it—and the Sheik looks happy with us. So he gets up from his cushion and he goes over to his needle box and takes out this paper and gives it to us. And that's how we find out about this here 'Shield of Agamemnon.'

"The paper is a map, you see. Follow it and it takes you to the old temple ruins, which everybody knows about, anyway. But this map shows you whereabouts to dig there to find the shield. You ever heard of the 'Shield of Agamemnon'?"

I shook my head.

"He was a Greek fellow, this Agamemnon. They all heard of him over there. Anyway, this map shows where to find his shield, and then the Sheik tells us that whoever has the Shield of this here Agamemnon . . . It's a Greek shield, ya know. Old. Real old. Has something to do with Helen of Troy. You ever heard of her?"

The name seemed vaguely familiar to me, and I nodded.

"'Whoever finds this shield will unite Arabia and slay its enemies!' the Sheik tells us. So we drink some more coffee—sip it, like. Then the Sheik goes to put the map back, and Larry leans over to me and grabs my arm hard. I can tell he's all excited.

"'There's money in it,' he whispers.

"So we sips some more coffee and then we asks to buy the map, but the Sheik says no, he can't sell it, because it's a sacred map. It goes right back to Helen of Troy.

"'But you can make a copy of it for fifty centimes,' the Sheik says.

"So Larry and I makes a copy of it, and we rents a motorcycle from Armand because we're in a hurry. It's the last day of our holiday, and we gotta get back to the war, you see."

The Hermit paused in his story and poured a dollop of whiskey into his tea. Then he poured the rest of the bottle into it. He took a sip and leaned back in the chair again. But he said nothing further. He seemed to have forgotten he was in the middle of the story.

"What about the shield?" I asked.

"Didn't find it. Couldn't even find the old temple ruins, and the motorcycle ran out of gas. We nearly died walking back. Forgot to take water, you see. It was just lucky that Armand came out there to see what happened to his motorcycle.

"Next time we come back to Rabat, we go right up to see the Sheik to get another copy of the map, 'cause we lost the first one. 'This time we'll get that darned shield!' Larry says. 'We'll rent a couple of camels and take some water with us.'

"Anyway, we go up to see the Sheik, and he's gone and died. They got a new Sheik, and he don't know nuthin' about the Shield of Agamemnon, but he wants to sell us a map to where the Chalice is buried. You ever heard about the Last Supper?"

I nodded. That was something I'd heard about.

"Anyway, we ain't going to bite on that. 'It's probably a fake,' Larry says. 'You don't get a map to the Chalice for fifty centimes,' he says."

He closed his eyes for a time. When he opened them and saw me sitting on his cot, the Hermit seemed surprised.

"You want another biscuit?" he asked.

I shook my head. "I can't stay," I said. "I'm looking for Pat."

"Good-bye, then," he said. "Come again. There's lots more smoked fish where those ones came from."

"Good-bye," I said. But he was already falling asleep and didn't hear me.

The beautiful day was still there when I stepped outside.

As I was wandering back along the creek, I saw a bald eagle high up in the sky. I wished I could be him for just a few minutes. From up there I would be able to spot my brother.

"Pat! Pat! Pat!" I shouted.

I stopped at the big pond on the way back and threw myself down on the bank to rest. I was exhausted, and it was relaxing just to lie there and stare at the clouds while I digested my fish. They were just ordinary clouds. I looked all around the sky, but they were all the same, just fluffy bits of sheep's wool floating up there in the blue sky. Except that far over, in the west, I thought I could see clouds that were darker. I hoped they would come our way and bring lightning and thunder. I felt like a storm.

I looked at the far clouds again. I thought I saw just the vaguest outline of something. A tornado? Was it? Yes, it might be. And it might come and lift our house away and flatten our barn. Then we could move back to Wistola. But I didn't feel like moving anywhere right then. It was such a lovely day. I could hear a meadowlark singing somewhere, over by the fence. I answered him. The Sergeant had taught me how to whistle, and I'd taught myself how to imitate a meadowlark.

It occurred to me that the Sergeant had taught me quite a few things. I whistled at the meadowlark again, and I closed my eyes to listen for a return call, but there was none.

When I opened my eyes, I could not decide whether or not I'd been sleeping. I thought not, but then I noticed that Bounce was fast asleep beside me. I looked at the sky. The sun seemed to be farther away than before, but I wasn't sure.

"Pat!" I yelled.

As I followed the creek to the east, I really began to

wonder where he could have gotten to. I didn't really expect to find him along this part of the creek. We seldom went here. It was the part that was too close to home.

I followed the creek across the half-quarter wheat field, right up to the road, then I crawled up a wooden piling to the top of the bridge and walked to the other side.

"Pat!" I called. "P—a—a—a—t!"

I noticed I was getting hoarse, so I wandered back down to the creek and sipped some water. A garter snake moved in the grass beside my head. I looked at it, and it looked at me, and for just a moment right then, I seemed to understand what it was like to be a garter snake.

"Have you seen Pat?" I asked.

After the green coolness of the creek, the road was hot and dusty, and I suddenly felt tired.

A little way past the slough, I ran into Catherine Schneider. She was on horseback, and she seemed to be surrounded by a golden haze. She rode out of the ditch and up to me. I looked into her eyes and saw a thousand glittering stars.

"I'm looking for Pat," I said.

"Pat? I haven't seen him," she said. "Want a ride back?"

She helped me up, and I sat on the horse's rump, behind the saddle. I held on to her and stared up into her golden hair, and my heart went *thumpety-thump* with the horse's hooves all the way back. Catherine deposited me on my doorstep and rode off. I stood there for a long time, feeling enjoyably dizzy. Then I sighed and went in.

"I couldn't find him," I said to Mother.

She was at the table, darning socks. She stared at me. "What?"

"Pat," I said. "I couldn't find him. I looked everywhere."

"He was sleeping upstairs," she said.

"I don't want any lunch," I said.

"Lunch!" she exclaimed. "Do you know what time it is?"

"No," I replied.

"It's seven o'clock," she said. "Supper was half an hour ago. Now you sit down there and you tell me where you've been for the last five hours!"

"I was looking for Pat," I said.

"Oh Lord!" she said.

I noticed that there was a large pan of baked macaroni and cheese on the back of the stove! It was my favorite food. I could eat it even when I wasn't hungry.

"Can I have some supper?" I asked.

"Where's Dad?" I asked a moment later, as I shoveled the macaroni into my mouth.

Mother looked at me from across the table.

"The last time I saw him, he said he was going to try along the creek," she answered.

"Try what?" I asked.

"Try looking for you there," she said.

After I'd had my supper, she sent me off to look for the Sergeant.

I headed up the creek, with the dog bouncing along beside me.

"We'll try the big pond," I said.

Much to my surprise, that's where he was. But he didn't seem to be looking for me. In fact, he was asleep on the bank, on the sunny side of the pond. He'd been for a swim. His hair was still wet, and his shorts were drying on the bushes.

He opened his eyes and looked up at me, as though he were trying to remember who I was.

After he got dressed, we sat together on the bank for a while and looked at the sky. It was still a warm and pleasant day.

"You know we're pretty far behind on our . . ." He hesitated, then started again. "What I mean is . . . Well, you know we've got a beautiful crop of wheat this year."

"I know," I said.

"So, things are looking good. There's only one thing. You know farming is . . . farming is a risky business. You could lose everything with a bad hailstorm. Or . . . I'll be plain. If this crop doesn't come in, we'll lose the farm."

I heard what he said, but it didn't quite register with me. Lose the farm? How could we lose the farm, just when I was finally getting used to it? The idea took me totally by surprise.

Good-bye, Miss Scott. Good-bye, Rachel. Good-bye, Charlie. Good-bye, trees and fields and grass and pond and creek. Good-bye, old hermit. Good-bye . . . everything. No, it didn't register. What he said just didn't register.

"Now it's not going to happen," he said, "but I wanted to warn you, just in case."

I looked at him, and he smiled at me.

"Whatever happens, you've been a great help to your mother and me, and we appreciate it.

"Come on, we'd better get home," he said, patting me on my back. He stood up and took out his brass watch and looked at it.

As we walked alongside the creek, he told me a story about how he spent two weeks in the snow, completely surrounded by Nazis. The story reminded me of something.

"Dad?"

"Yeah?"

"Can I shoot the gun now?"

"Sorry, pal, I sold it a long time ago," he said. He smiled and patted me on the shoulder.

As we climbed up the bank of the creek and started across the pasture, my legs felt like a pair of lead posts, and I was suddenly very weary. No wonder in that, for I'd spent the entire day walking all over the place, first searching for Pat and then searching for the Sergeant.

In order to take my mind off my tired bones, I looked up at the sky and examined the summery clouds as we went forward. I was fond of clouds, because they can be very pretty—when they're behaving themselves.

I looked down again, beyond the pasture, and I saw the wheat fields glimmering like a golden sea. In the distance I saw the barn and the chicken coop and the outhouse and all the other familiar buildings. Finally, through the trees, I caught a glimpse of our house, and I felt a small thrill of relief and happiness. I would soon be there. I was nearly home.

When we were passing by the barn, I asked him to wait a minute, and I went inside and climbed up to the loft. When I came back, I gave him my ten dollars.

"It's for the mortgage," I said.

The Sergeant then did a strange thing. He lifted me off the ground, and he hugged me tightly, until I could hardly breathe.

After he put me down, we both heard Mother's voice ring out in the distance, on the far side of the trees, in the direction of the creek.

"Edward! Donald!" she yelled harshly. "Where are you? Answer me!"

"It's Mother," I said. "She's looking for us. She sounds pretty mad."

"Don't worry about it," Father said quietly. "We'll send Pat after her."